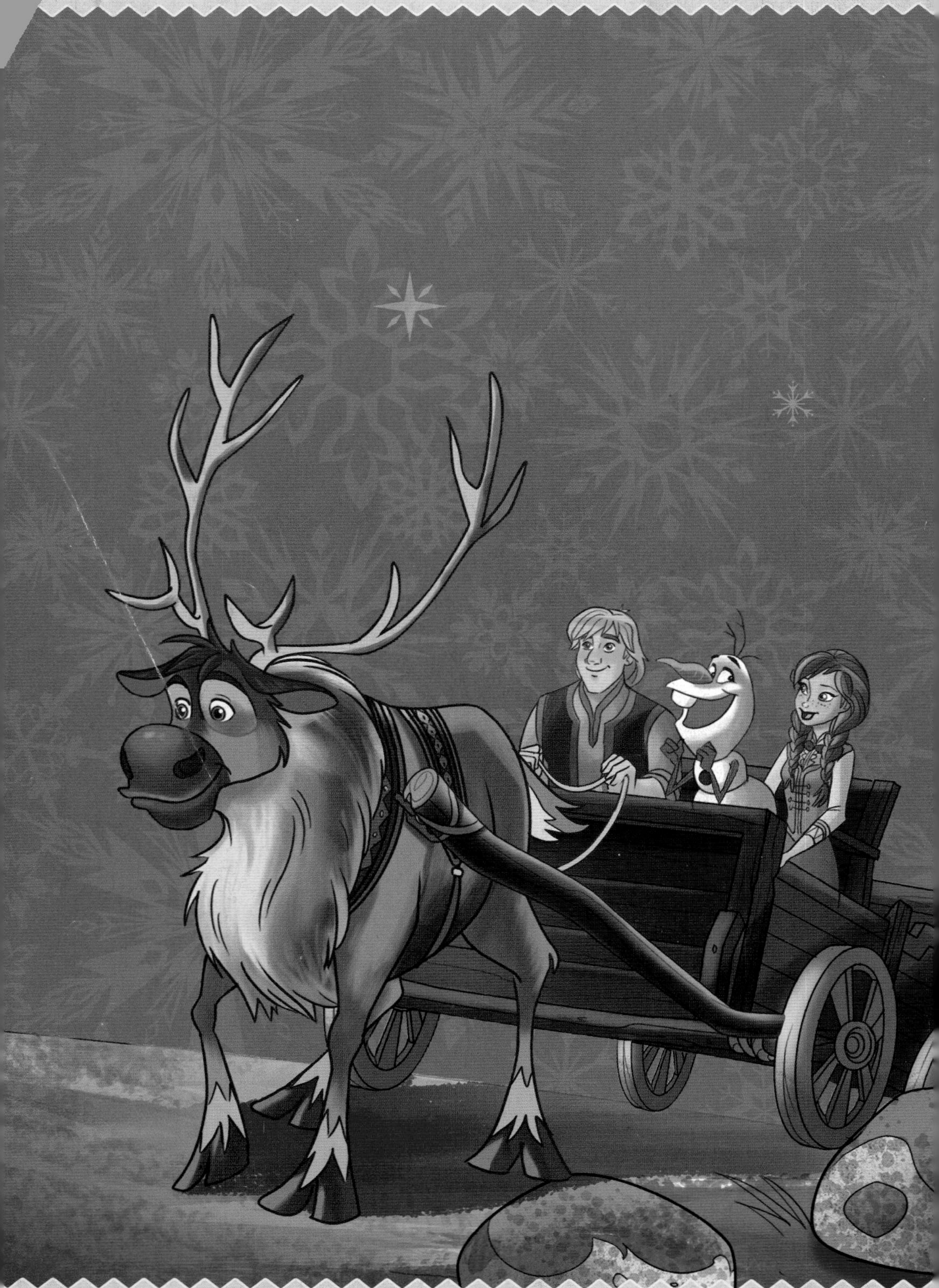

Disney

FROZEN

ADVENTURES

Flurries
of Fun

DARK HORSE BOOKS

DARK HORSE BOOKS

PRESIDENT AND PUBLISHER
MIKE RICHARDSON

COLLECTION EDITOR
FREDDYE MILLER

DESIGNER
SARAH TERRY

COLLECTION ASSISTANT EDITOR
JUDY KHUU

DIGITAL ART TECHNICIAN
SAMANTHA HUMMER

Neil Hankerson Executive Vice President **Tom Weddle** Chief Financial Officer **Randy Stradley** Vice President of Publishing **Nick McWhorter** Chief Business Development Officer **Dale LaFountain** Chief Information Officer **Matt Parkinson** Vice President of Marketing **Cara Niece** Vice President of Production and Scheduling **Mark Bernardi** Vice President of Book Trade and Digital Sales **Ken Lizzi** General Counsel **Dave Marshall** Editor in Chief **Davey Estrada** Editorial Director **Chris Warner** Senior Books Editor **Cary Grazzini** Director of Specialty Projects **Lia Ribacchi** Art Director **Vanessa Todd-Holmes** Director of Print Purchasing **Matt Dryer** Director of Digital Art and Prepress **Michael Gombos** Senior Director of International Publishing and Licensing **Kari Yadro** Director of Custom Programs **Kari Torson** Director of International Licensing **Sean Brice** Director of Trade Sales

DISNEY PUBLISHING WORLDWIDE GLOBAL MAGAZINES, COMICS AND PARTWORKS

PUBLISHER **Lynn Waggoner** • EDITORIAL TEAM **Bianca Coletti** (Director, Magazines), **Guido Frazzini** (Director, Comics), **Carlotta Quattrocolo** (Executive Editor), **Stefano Ambrosio** (Executive Editor, New IP), **Camilla Vedove** (Senior Manager, Editorial Development), **Behnoosh Khalili** (Senior Editor), **Julie Dorris** (Senior Editor), **Mina Riazi** (Assistant Editor), **Jonathan Manning** (Assistant Editor) • DESIGN **Enrico Soave** (Senior Designer) • ART **Ken Shue** (VP, Global Art), **Manny Mederos** (Senior Illustration Manager, Comics and Magazines), **Roberto Santillo** (Creative Director), **Marco Ghiglione** (Creative Manager), **Stefano Attardi** (Illustration Manager) • PORTFOLIO MANAGEMENT **Olivia Ciancarelli** (Director) • BUSINESS & MARKETING **Mariantonietta Galla** (Senior Manager, Franchise), **Virpi Korhonen** (Editorial Manager)

FROZEN ADVENTURES: FLURRIES OF FUN

Published by Dark Horse Books
A division of Dark Horse Comics LLC
10956 SE Main Street, Milwaukie, OR 97222

DarkHorse.com

To find a comics shop in your area, visit comicshoplocator.com

First edition: September 2019 | ISBN 978-1-50671-470-7
Digital ISBN 978-1-50671-473-8

10 9 8 7 6 5 4 3 2 1
Printed in China

THE SHIFTING SHORES OF SANKERSHUS

Script: Georgia Ball; Layouts: Benedetta Barone; Inks: Veronica Di Lorenzo; Colors: Cecilia Giumento, Manuela Nerolini; Kat Maximenko, Julia Pinchuk, Hanna Chinstova, Nastia Beloushova; Letters: AndWorld Design

Sankershus, early Summer.

"I AM ELSA, QUEEN OF ARENDELLE. I HAVE ICE POWERS!"

"I AM GOOD AND KIND AND EVERYONE IS WELCOME INSIDE MY CASTLE..."

NIKLAS! YOU'RE WRECKING MY KINGDOM!

DON'T MIND HIM, MARIT. THE WEATHER IS MAKING HIM RESTLESS.

AS SOON AS THE RAIN STOPS I'M GOING TO BURY THESE STONES WITH THE REST OF MY TREASURE WHERE NO LITTLE BROTHER WILL EVER FIND THEM.

I DON'T LIKE HOW LONG THIS RAIN'S BEEN FALLING--

--OR HOW HEAVY IT'S BEEN COMING DOWN.

IT'S BEEN POURING FOR DAYS. THE RIVER IS RISING AND I'M WORRIED THERE'LL BE FLOODING. I'M GOING OUT TO HAVE A LOOK AROUND, TILIA.

DON'T BE LONG! DINNER WILL BE READY SOON.

While the Skiftende River rises...

Two days later, the sun shines brightly over Arendelle-- on Midsummer's Day!

OLAF, COME HELP US MAKE FLOWER CROWNS FOR MIDSUMMER!

OH, I *LOVE* FLOWER CROWNS! I WANT TO MAKE ONE...

OK, WE'LL SHOW YOU HOW!

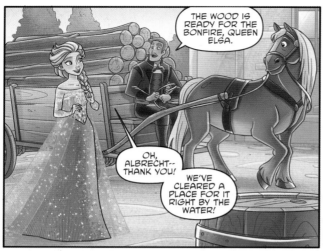

THE WOOD IS READY FOR THE BONFIRE, QUEEN ELSA.

OH, ALBRECHT-- THANK YOU!

WE'VE CLEARED A PLACE FOR IT RIGHT BY THE WATER!

WHAT DO YOU THINK OF THE WREATHS THIS YEAR, PRINCESS ANNA?

GORGEOUS! ARE THOSE HYACINTHS, ELKE?

MMM-HMM...

ELSA! ANNA! CAN YOU COME TO THE DOCK?

WHAT IS IT, KRISTOFF?

I JUST THOUGHT YOU MIGHT LIKE TO SEE THE BOATS!

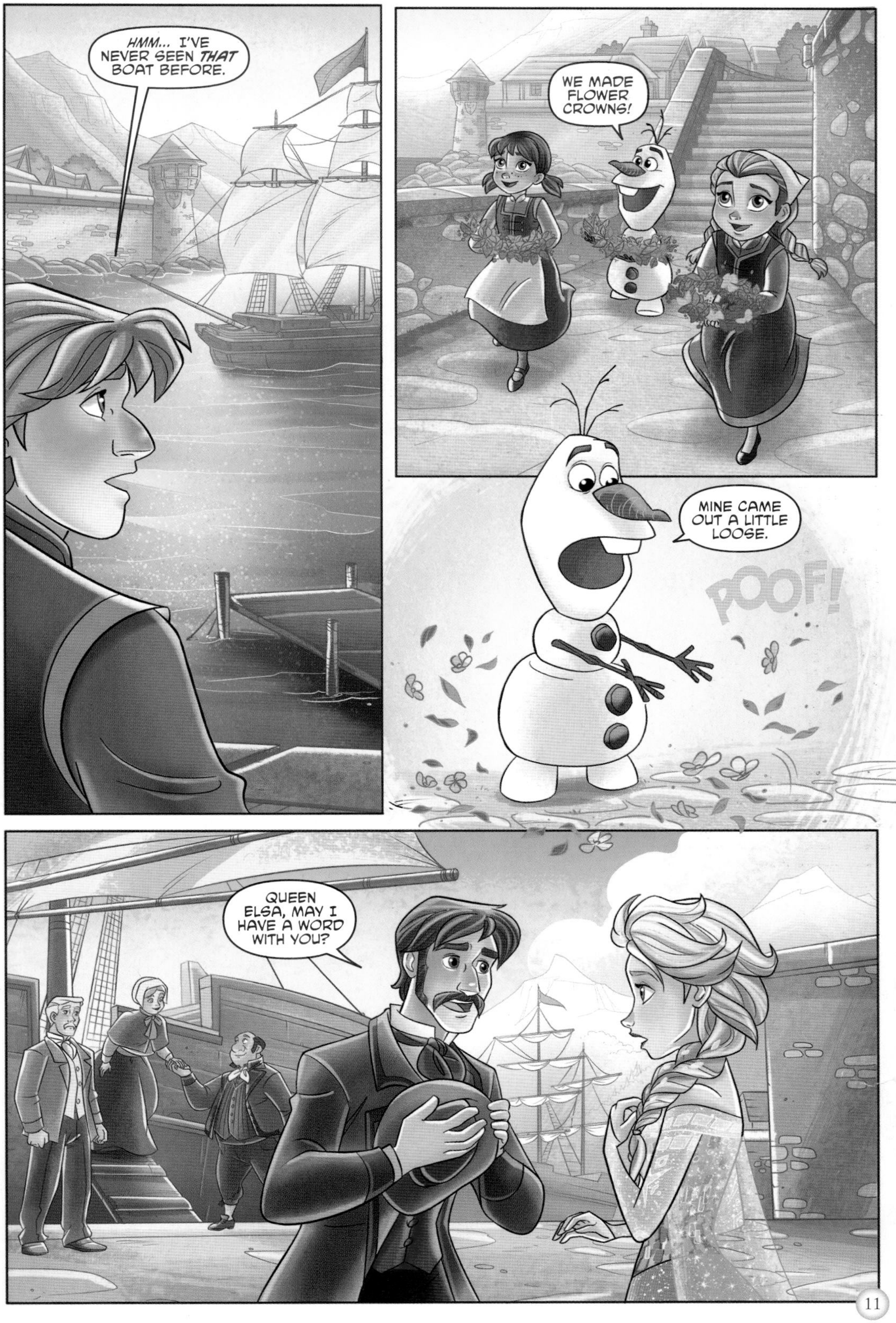
HMM... I'VE NEVER SEEN *THAT* BOAT BEFORE.
WE MADE FLOWER CROWNS!
MINE CAME OUT A LITTLE LOOSE.
POOF!
QUEEN ELSA, MAY I HAVE A WORD WITH YOU?

MY NAME IS KLAUS, AND MY FRIENDS AND I HAVE COME FROM SANKERSHUS.

OH MY, YOU'VE COME A LONG WAY!

AS YOU KNOW, SANKERSHUS IS NORTHEAST ALONG THE SKIFTENDE RIVER, AT LEAST A DAY'S JOURNEY AWAY BY BOAT.

WE'VE LIVED THERE ALL OUR LIVES, AS OUR ANCESTORS DID BEFORE US.

IT MUST BE SERIOUS IF YOU'VE TRAVELED SO FAR DURING MIDSUMMER CELEBRATIONS! WHAT CAN WE DO TO HELP?

"WE'VE HAD A LOT OF RAIN IN RECENT YEARS. SOMETIMES THE RIVER SWELLED SO MUCH IT NEARLY REACHED THE HOMES ON ITS SHORE, BUT NOW THEIR FLOORS ARE UNDERWATER.

"THE RIVER'S BEEN SWELLING MORE OFTEN AND SOON THE WHOLE VILLAGE MAY FLOOD. THE GROUND IS SOFT AND SATURATED WITH WATER AND THE MOUNTAINSIDE COULD COLLAPSE.

"I THINK IT MAY BE TIME TO FIND A SAFER PLACE TO LIVE."

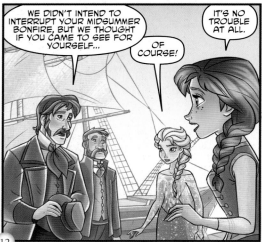

WE DIDN'T INTEND TO INTERRUPT YOUR MIDSUMMER BONFIRE, BUT WE THOUGHT IF YOU CAME TO SEE FOR YOURSELF...

OF COURSE!

IT'S NO TROUBLE AT ALL.

WE'LL LEAVE AT ONCE!

I'LL SEE THAT A BOAT IS PREPARED, QUEEN ELSA.

After two days on the river, Klaus leads Elsa and Anna through Sankershus...

AS YOU CAN SEE, QUEEN ELSA...

...IT DOESN'T LOOK GOOD.

I DON'T LIKE THE ANGLE OF THOSE TREES ON THE HILL...

THERE COULD BE A MUDSLIDE ANY DAY NOW. WE NEED TO DO SOMETHING RIGHT AWAY!

I THINK YOU ALREADY KNOW WHAT I'M GOING TO SAY?

I THINK I DO.

IF THE HILLS COME DOWN, OUR HOMES WILL BE BURIED... THE MUD WILL BE TOO THICK AND THE GROUND TOO UNSTABLE TO BUILD ON AGAIN.

IT'S TOO DANGEROUS TO LIVE IN A SETTLEMENT HERE ANY LONGER-- SANKERSHUS WILL HAVE TO BE MOVED!

BUT WE WILL DO EVERYTHING WE CAN TO ASSIST YOU!

"WE'LL FIND A NEW AND SAFE LOCATION FOR YOUR VILLAGE--"

"WE'LL MAKE TRIPS TO RETRIEVE YOUR LIVESTOCK AND ALL OF YOUR PERSONAL POSSESSIONS."

"AND HELP YOU BUILD NEW HOMES THERE FOR EACH OF YOUR FAMILIES.

"UNTIL THE WORK IS DONE..."

"...THERE'S PLENTY OF ROOM FOR YOU IN ARENDELLE."

Arendelle, two weeks later.

ONE... TWO... THREE...

THERE YOU ARE!

AW, HOW DID YOU FIND ME SO FAST?

And another game of hide-and-seek...

WOW, YOU GUYS ARE REALLY GOOD AT THIS...

And another...

ARE YOU SURE YOU WEREN'T PEEKING?

COME ON, LET'S PLAY AGAIN!

MARIT?

WHY AREN'T YOU PLAYING HIDE-AND-SEEK WITH US?

I MISS HOME TOO MUCH TO PLAY.

ELSA!

MARIT MISSES HER OLD HOME, AND IT'S MAKING HER TOO SAD TO PLAY WITH US...

...CAN YOU MAKE HER HAPPY AGAIN?

I'LL DO MY BEST...

WHAT'S WRONG, MARIT?

WELL...

THE CASTLE IS REALLY PRETTY...

AND EVERYONE'S BEEN SO NICE TO US! BUT...

BUT YOU CAN'T STOP THINKING ABOUT SANKERSHUS?

I KNOW WE'RE GOING TO HAVE NEW HOMES, BUT I'VE LIVED BY THE RIVER MY WHOLE LIFE. I'M AFRAID I WON'T BE HAPPY IN A NEW PLACE.

HAVE YOU EVER FELT LIKE THAT?

I THINK I HAVE.

"I LEFT HOME ONCE, AND I THOUGHT I WAS NEVER GOING BACK."

"THE MOUNTAINS WERE STRANGE AND UNFAMILIAR..."

"SO I *MADE* THEM FAMILIAR."

"I FOUND WAYS TO TURN A NEW PLACE INTO SOMETHING THAT FELT LIKE HOME.

"BUT I REALLY BELONGED IN ARENDELLE WITH MY FRIENDS AND MY FAMILY, BECAUSE YOUR HOME IS WITH THE PEOPLE YOU LOVE--

"--NOT A PLACE."

YOU MADE A PALACE OUT OF ICE? I HOPE I GET TO SEE IT SOME DAY!

I'LL MAKE SURE YOU DO. I PROMISE.

THE BOATS ARE READY, QUEEN ELSA. WE SHOULD LEAVE FOR SANKERSHUS AGAIN WHILE THE WEATHER HOLDS UP.

Sänkershus, two days later.

Elsa and Anna return to Sänkershus with a small group of villagers one last time to retrieve the rest of their possessions...

MAMA STAYED IN ARENDELLE TO TAKE CARE OF NIKLAS. I PROMISED HER I'D BRING BACK HER ROSETTE IRON.* IT WILL HELP HER GET USED TO OUR NEW HOME TO HAVE SOMETHING THAT BELONGED TO *HER* MOTHER.

THEN WE WON'T LEAVE WITHOUT IT!

THIS WAY, PRINCESS ANNA!

I SHOULD BRING SOMETHING THAT WILL MAKE MY NEW HOME FEEL FAMILIAR TO *ME*...BUT I'M NOT SURE WHAT...

*A ROSETTE IRON IS A MOLD WITH AN INTRICATE DESIGN USED TO MAKE A DEEP-FRIED HOLIDAY PASTRY DIPPED IN SUGAR!

ROSETTE IRON, HMM...

I KNOW! MY TREASURE BAG!

I THINK I REMEMBER WHERE IT IS...

WHAT WAS THAT, MARIT?

FOUND IT!

ANNA! WE HAVE TO LEAVE, THE VILLAGE IS GOING TO FLOOD!

WE CAN'T GO JUST YET, MARIT HAS RUN OFF!

MARIT?

WHERE HAS SHE GONE?

I DON'T KNOW--I HEARD SOMETHING ABOUT TREASURE?

HER LITTLE BAG OF STONES! I THINK SHE BURIED IT IN A HOLE UP ON THE HILLSIDE...

WE'LL FIND HER, KLAUS.

KRISTOFF!

THE RAIN'S MAKING IT HARD TO SEE--ARE YOU SURE YOU DON'T WANT TO GO BACK TO THE BOATS NOW?

NOT WITHOUT MARIT! BUT LET'S GET EVERYONE ELSE ON BOARD SAFELY.

BE CAREFUL! THAT RIVER IS RISING FAST...

CRACKLE

STAND BACK...

WHY? WHAT ARE YOU GOING TO--?

SHOOOSH

EVERYTHING WE HEARD IS TRUE-- AMAZING!

ISN'T IT?

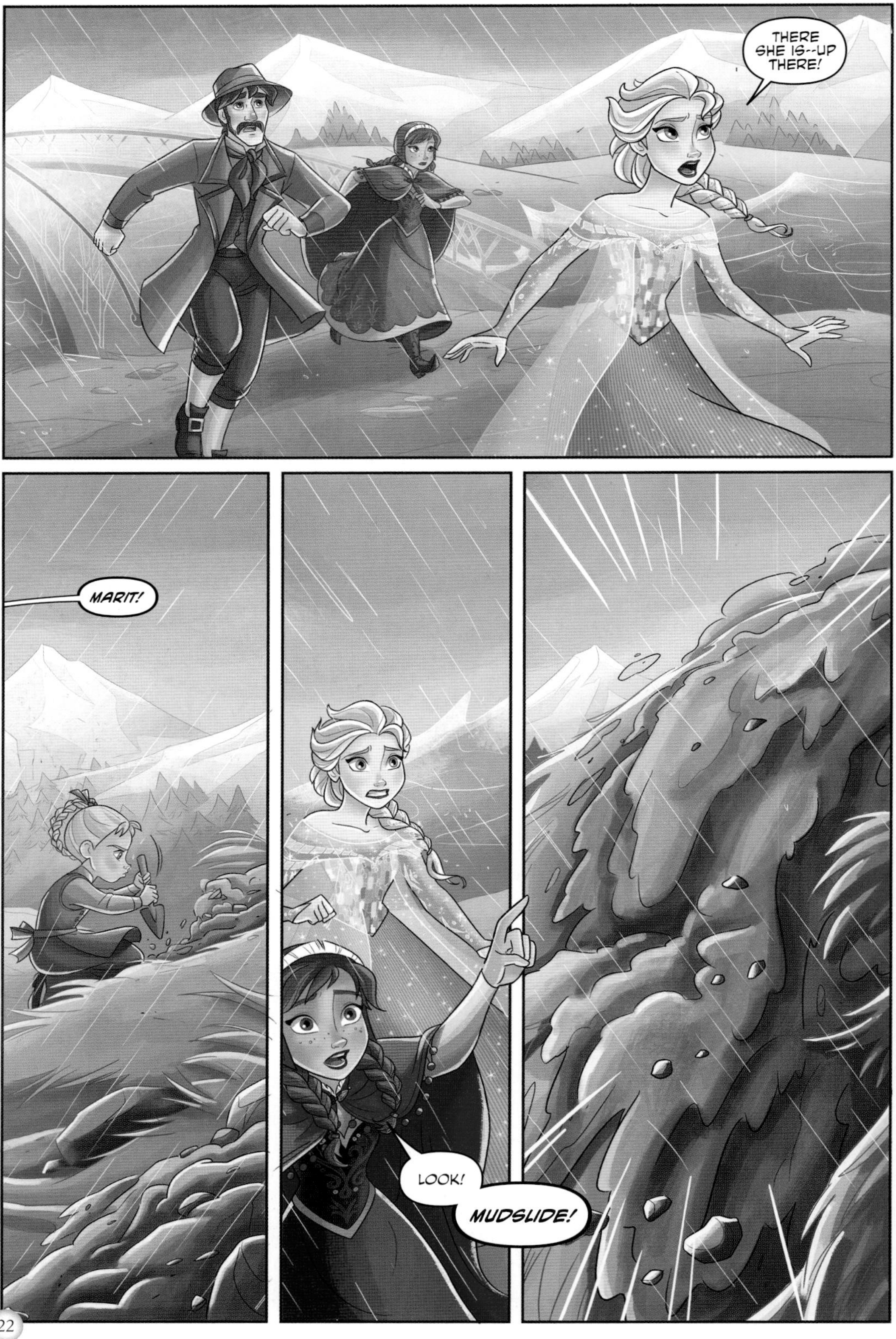
THERE SHE IS--UP THERE!
MARIT!
LOOK!
MUDSLIDE!

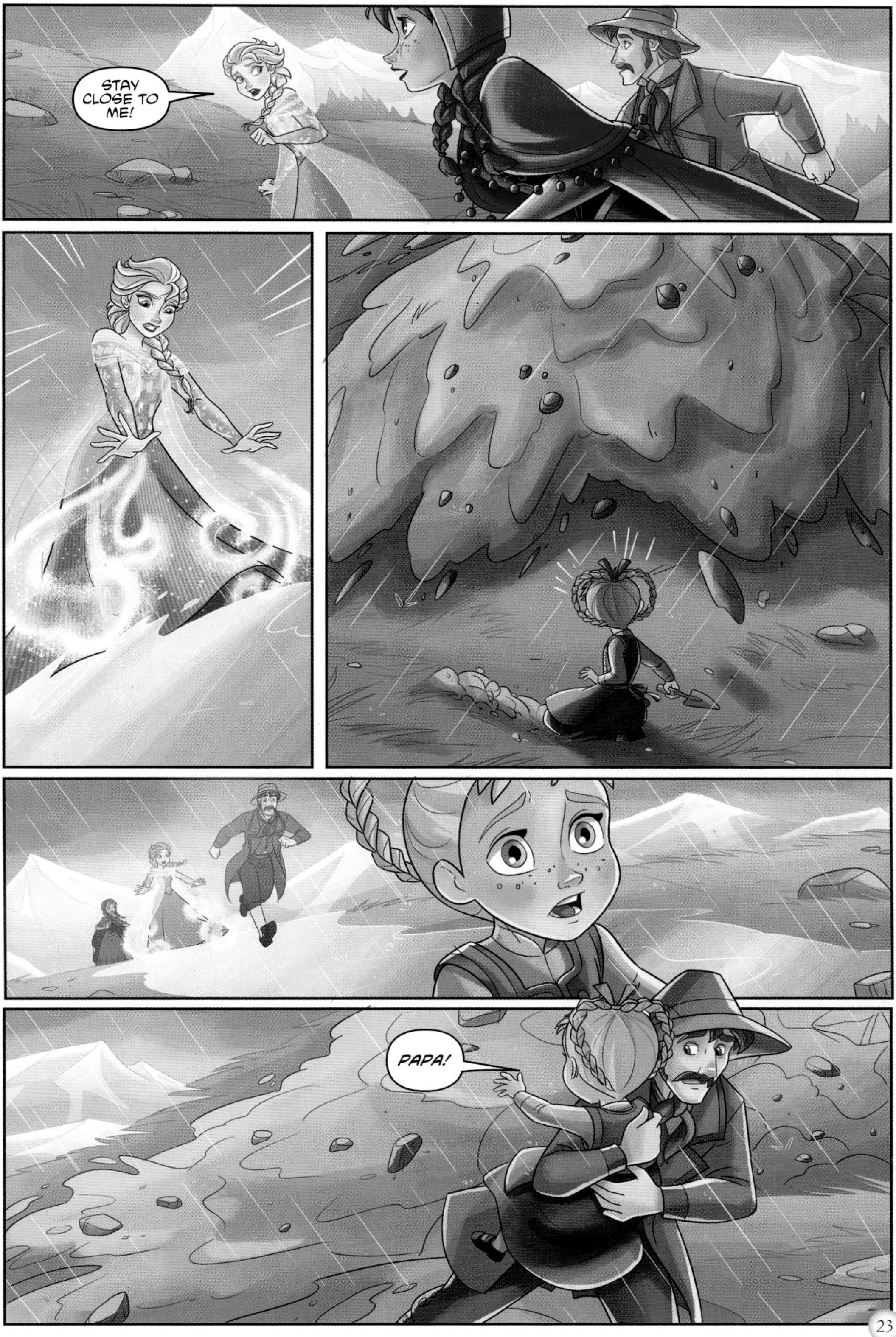
STAY CLOSE TO ME!
PAPA!

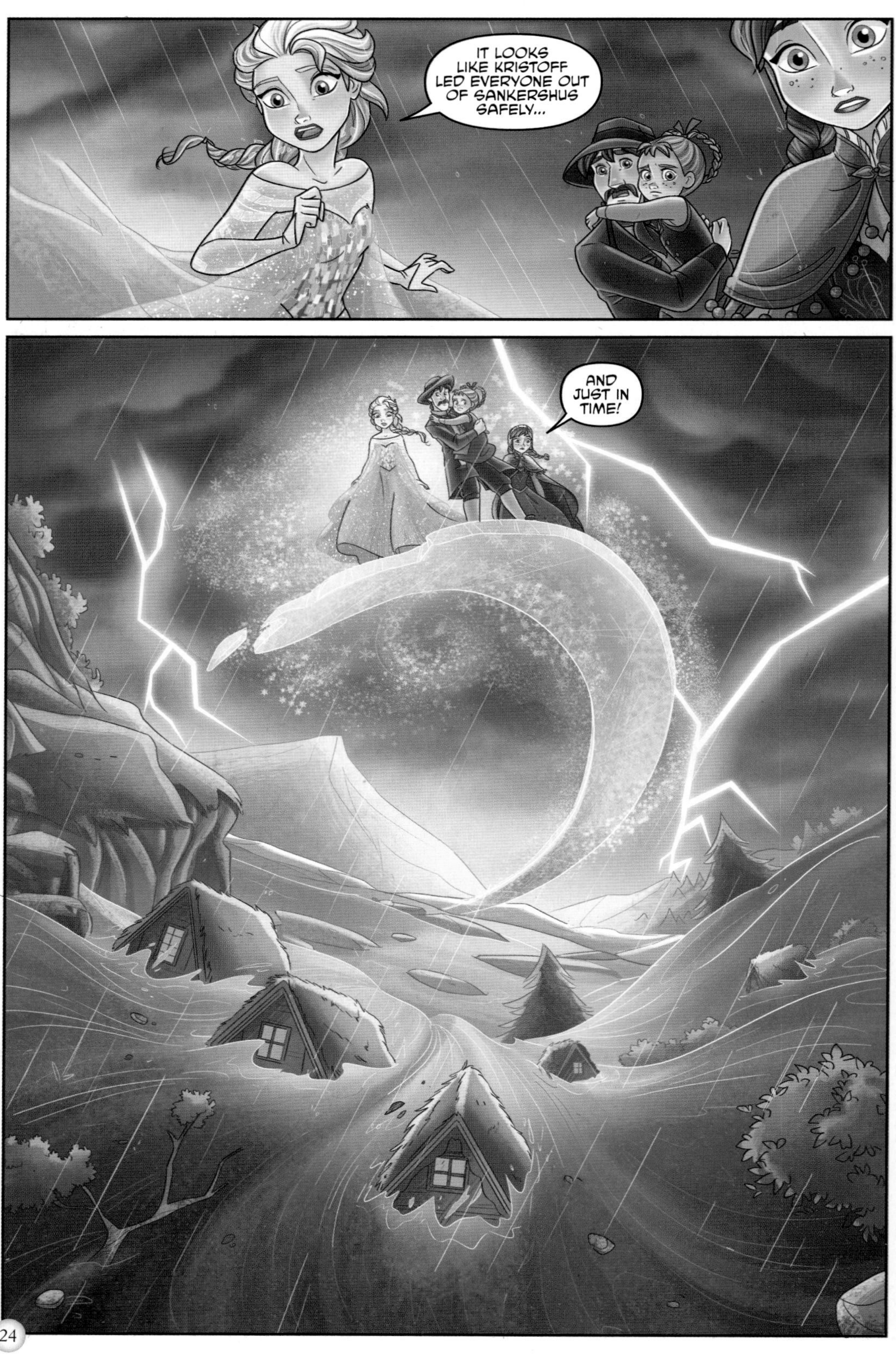
IT LOOKS LIKE KRISTOFF LED EVERYONE OUT OF SANKERSHUS SAFELY...
AND JUST IN TIME!

I COULD MAKE AN ICE WALL BETWEEN THE HOUSES AND THE RIVER IF YOU WOULD LIKE MORE TIME.

THANK YOU, QUEEN ELSA... BUT I THINK THAT WOULD ONLY DELAY THE INEVITABLE. BESIDES--

--WE HAVE EVERYTHING WE NEED.

GOOD-BYE, SANKERSHUS.

I FOUND YOUR MOTHER'S ROSETTE IRON, MARIT...

BUT I'M SORRY WE COULDN'T SAVE YOUR BAG OF TREASURE.

THAT'S OK.

I'LL MISS MY RIVER STONES, AND I'LL MISS OUR OLD HOUSE.

BUT I HAVE MY FAMILY, AND MY NEW FRIENDS IN ARENDELLE!

NOW I CAN'T WAIT TO SEE THE TREASURES I'LL FIND IN MY NEW HOME.

A few days later, in Arendelle...

As the new village nears completion, Arendelle celebrates Midsummer's Day a few weeks later than originally planned...

WHICH WAY ARE WE GOING AGAIN? I THOUGHT WE WENT *THAT* WAY LAST TIME...

I'M GLAD WE POSTPONED MIDSUMMER'S DAY UNTIL THE NEW HOMES WERE FINISHED SO WE COULD ALL CELEBRATE TOGETHER!

I HOPE THERE ARE MANY MORE CELEBRATIONS LIKE IT AHEAD OF US.

CHILDREN! TIME TO GO!

YAY!

YAY!

YAY!

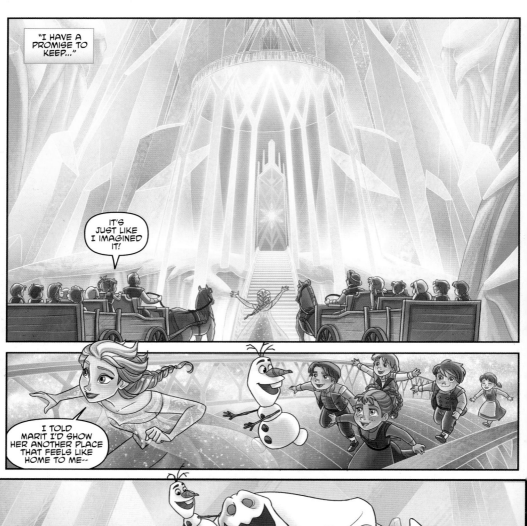

"I HAVE A PROMISE TO KEEP..."

IT'S JUST LIKE I IMAGINED IT!

I TOLD MARIT I'D SHOW HER ANOTHER PLACE THAT FEELS LIKE HOME TO ME--

--BECAUSE IT'S FILLED WITH MY DEAREST FRIENDS!

The End

SAILING SISTERS

IT'S ANOTHER BEAUTIFUL SUNNY DAY IN ARENDELLE...

BUT TODAY SOMETHING SPECIAL IS ABOUT TO HAPPEN...

DO YOU THINK WE'VE PACKED ENOUGH?

THIS IS EXCITING! I HAVE NEVER BEEN ON A ROYAL TRIP!

NOR HAVE I! AND THE BEST THING IS...

THAT WE ARE TRAVELING BY SHIP!

THE KINGDOM OF VAKRETTA IS WAITING FOR US!

Manuscript: Tea Orsi; Layout: Nicoletta Baldari; Cleanup: Nicoletta Baldari; Color: Dario Calabria

I NEED ONE LAST **WARM** HUG!

SURE!

HERE'S A BIG ONE FOR YOU!

IT WILL KEEP YOU WARM UNTIL WE GET BACK!

BE CAREFUL ON THAT SHIP!

YEAH! I CAN'T WAIT TO TAKE THE WHEEL!

WHAT?!? YOU'LL BE DRIVING?

I PROMISE I'LL BE VEEERY CAREFUL!

HAVE A SAFE JOURNEY!

COME BACK SOON!

WE WILL! BYE!

CAN I TAKE THE WHEEL?

OF COURSE!

IS THE KINGDOM OF VAKRETTA REALLY FAR?

NOT SO FAR, YOUR MAJESTY!

WE'LL BE THERE IN ABOUT TWO DAYS!

I LOOK FORWARD TO IT!

ELSA AND ANNA TRAVEL ALL THROUGH THE NIGHT...

AND DAY...

WOO, HOO! I LOVE SAILING!

YOU'RE GREAT, CAPTAIN ANNA!

BUT WHEN THEY REACH THE KINGDOM OF VAKRETTA...

WHERE IS EVERYONE?

THIS IS STRANGE! THEY KNEW WE WERE ARRIVING TODAY!

THEN ELSA SPOTS SOMEONE...

I CAN'T BELIEVE IT!

IS THAT THE DUKE OF WESELTON?

WHAT IS HE DOING HERE? WE'RE SO FAR FROM HIS HOME...

THE DUKE WAS VERY UNKIND TO ELSA WHEN HER FROZEN GIFTS WERE FIRST REVEALED...

I AM VISITING
MY MOTHER'S COUSIN'S
WIFE'S NEPHEW IF YOU
MUST KNOW.

I WOULD
LEAVE RIGHT **NOW**
IF I WERE YOU!

VAKRETTA
IS HAVING THE
HOTTEST SUMMER
IN YEARS!

TAKE US
TO THE VILLAGE,
PLEASE!

THE DUKE IMMEDIATELY
LEADS THE SISTERS TO
THE VILLAGE...

POOR PEOPLE!
THEY LOOK SO **HOT**
AND TIRED!

WE MUST
HELP THEM!

YES, AND
I KNOW **WHAT**
TO DO!

YEAH?

33

A BIT OF **SNOW** WILL MAKE YOU FEEL BETTER!

HURRAY FOR QUEEN ELSA!

HUH?!?

SOON EVERYONE IS ENJOYING THE COLD...

SWISH

WELL.... **ALMOST** EVERYONE!

SWOOOSH

GASP!

YOU DEFINITELY HAVE THE **POWER** TO MAKE PEOPLE HAPPY, ELSA!

AND I LOVE IT!

The End

How to Beat the Heat

ANNA AND ELSA ARE TRAVELING TO CHATO...

IT'S SO HOT! AND THE SUN IS SO BRIGHT! IT'S SO... IT'S SO...

SUMMERY?

YES, OLAF, IT'S VERY SUMMERY!

I'VE GOT TO DO SOMETHING TO KEEP EVERYONE COOL IN THIS HEAT!

TAP
TAP

Manuscript: Tea Orsi; Layout: Alberto Zanon; Cleanup: Benedetta Barone; Color: MichelAngela World

HMMM... I'M NOT SURE THIS IS THE BEST IDEA.

WHOOOPS!

WHOAAAH!

YOU'RE RIGHT!

TAP
TAP

PHEEW!

KEEPING EVERYONE COOL IS HARDER THAN I THOUGHT IT WOULD BE!

SOMETIMES SUMMER BRINGS PROBLEMS, NOT JUST BEAUTIFUL WARM DAYS!

OH, NO! I LOVE SUMMER, AND THE SUN, AND EVERYTHING WARM... LIKE WARM HUGS!

I GOT IT! EVERYONE! HUG OLAF!

ELSA! YOU'RE A GENIUS!

COME HERE, BUDDY!

AWW, I LIKE YOU TOO!

NICE WORK, ELSA! WITH A BODY MADE OF SNOW AND HIS PERSONAL FLURRY, OLAF IS THE ONLY COLD THING ON THE SHIP!

WELL, WHO'S NEXT?

The End

Morning Bike Ride

Manuscript: Tea Orsi; Layout: Emilio Urbano; Cleanup: Veronica Di Lorenzo; Color: Dario Calabria

DON'T YOU REMEMBER? WE ARE GOING FOR A BIKE RIDE! OUR ANNUAL FIRST-DAY-OF-SPRING RIDE!

OH...YEAH!

I'M SO EXCITED!

I'LL GO AND GET THE BIKE. SEE YOU OUTSIDE!

OKAY! I'LL BE THERE IN A MINUTE!

OOPS! I THINK WE ARE A BIT EARLY...

YEAH. SO EARLY, IT'S STILL NIGHT!

I WAS SO EXCITED THAT I DIDN'T EVEN LOOK AT THE CLOCK!

WELL... AT LEAST NOW I KNOW HOW TO GET YOU UP EARLY!

The End

A Touch of Spring

Manuscript: Tea Orsi; Layout: Emilio Urbano; Cleanup: Rosa La Barbera; Color: Dario Calabria

The End

UNEXPECTED MASTERPIECE

Manuscript: Tea Orsi; Layout: Manuela Razzi; Clean up: Manuela Razzi; Color: Maria Claudia Di GEnova

The End

PARADE OF LIGHTS

ANNA, KRISTOFF AND OLAF ARE TRAVELLING TO TROLL VALLEY FOR SOME TROLL-SITTING!

I CAN'T WAIT TO PLAY WITH THE LITTLE TROLLS!

ME TOO! LAST TIME WE HAD SO MUCH FUN!

WHERE COULD HE BE?

HE'S SO LITTLE... HE CAN'T HAVE GONE FAR!

WHAT'S GOING ON?

ONE OF THE BABIES IS MISSING!

DON'T WORRY! WE'LL FIND HIM!

THANKS, KRISTOFF!

ANNA, KRISTOFF AND OLAF HELP SEARCHING FOR THE BABY...

MAYBE HE'S PLAYING HIDE-AND-SEEK!

OHHH!!!

Manuscript: Valentina Cambi; Layout: Alberto Zanon; Cleanup: Letizia Algeri; Color: MichelAngela World

WAIT, LITTLE FRIEND! I'LL COME WITH YOU!

KRISTOFF! LOOK! OLAF IS RUNNING AFTER A FIREFLY!

LET'S FOLLOW HIM!

WE NEED TO STAY FOCUSED ON FINDING EKON!

BUT MAYBE THE SAME CURIOSITY LURED AWAY THE BABY TROLL!

RIGHT! TROLLS ARE VERY INQUISITIVE!

ANNA AND HER FRIENDS FOLLOW THE LITTLE GLOWING INSECT. BUT IT'S NOT ALONE...

LOOK AT ALL HIS BROTHERS AND SISTERS!

AND THEY ALL LOOK LIKE THEY ARE GOING SOMEWHERE...

BUT WHERE?

A FEW STEPS LATER...

WHAT'S THAT LIGHT?

I DON'T KNOW, OLAF.

LET'S KEEP FOLLOWING THE FIREFLIES AND WE'LL FIND IT OUT!

ANNA, KRISTOFF AND OLAF FINALLY REACH THE CLEARING!

HA HA!

HERE HE IS! I'M SO RELIEVED!

NO WONDER HE CAME HERE... IT'S QUITE A SPECTACLE!

THEY'RE BRIGHTER THAN CANDLES AND LESS DANGEROUS! THEY WOULD BE PERFECT TO LIGHT UP MY BEDROOM! CAN WE BRING THEM ALL HOME?

The End

44

LET'S HELP OAKEN!

Manuscript: Tea Orsi; Layout: Elisabetta Melaranci; Cleanup: Manuela Razzi; Color: Dario Calabria

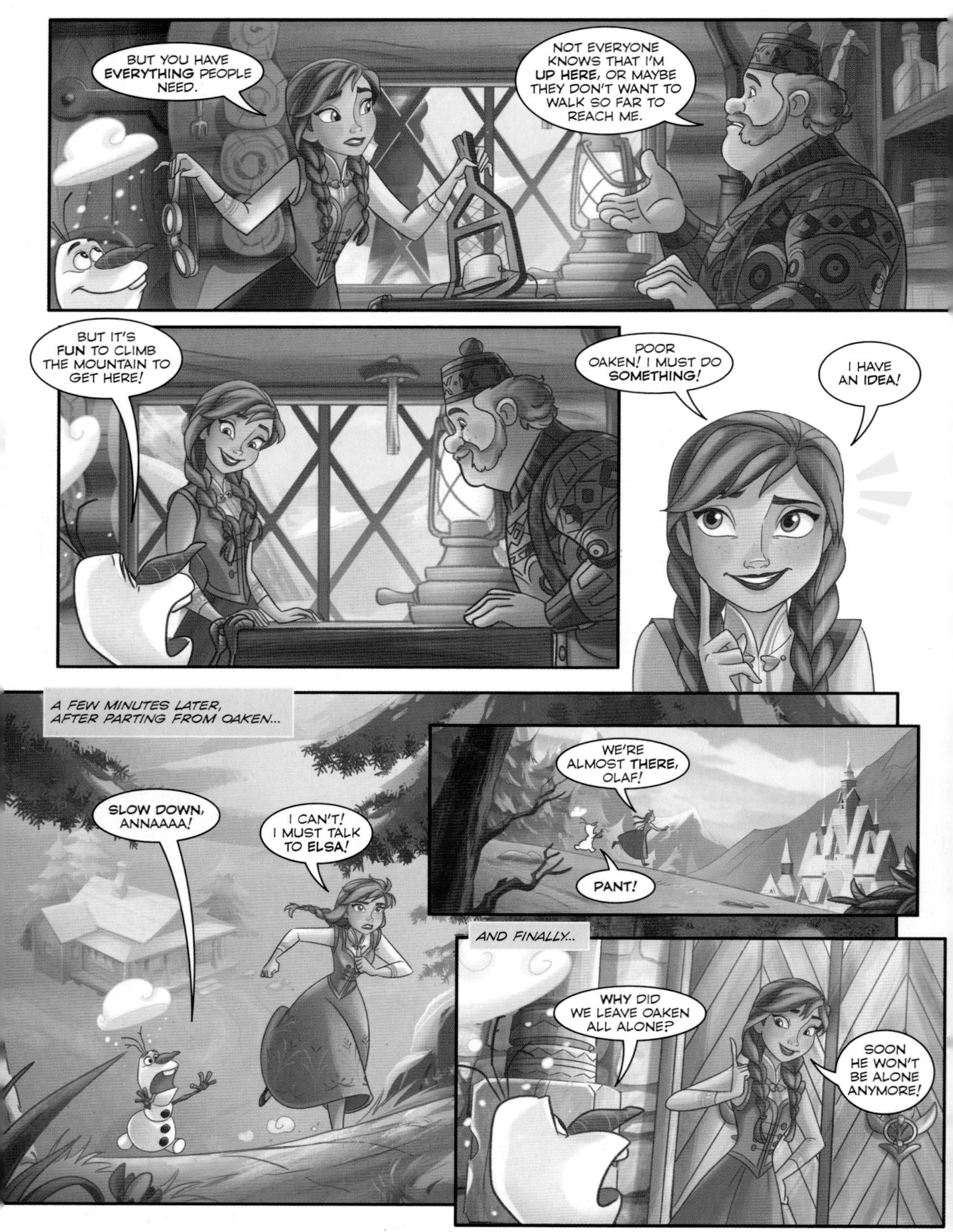
BUT YOU HAVE EVERYTHING PEOPLE NEED.
NOT EVERYONE KNOWS THAT I'M UP HERE, OR MAYBE THEY DON'T WANT TO WALK SO FAR TO REACH ME.
BUT IT'S FUN TO CLIMB THE MOUNTAIN TO GET HERE!
POOR OAKEN! I MUST DO SOMETHING!
I HAVE AN IDEA!
A FEW MINUTES LATER, AFTER PARTING FROM OAKEN...
SLOW DOWN, ANNAAAA!
I CAN'T! I MUST TALK TO ELSA!
WE'RE ALMOST THERE, OLAF!
PANT!
AND FINALLY...
WHY DID WE LEAVE OAKEN ALL ALONE?
SOON HE WON'T BE ALONE ANYMORE!

ANNA CALLS ELSA AND KRISTOFF TO TELL THEM ABOUT OAKEN'S STORE...

IF WE WORK TOGETHER, WE CAN TELL THE **ENTIRE** KINGDOM ABOUT OAKEN'S POST.

YOU'RE RIGHT!

GREAT IDEA!

BUT... HOW CAN WE DO THAT?

GOOD QUESTION!

HERE'S MY PLAN!

GASP!

WOW!

ANNA → BANNER!

OAKEN

I'LL MAKE SOME BIG BANNERS TO HANG IN THE STREETS!

ELSA, CAN YOU MAKE SOME ICE SCULPTURES THAT SHOW WHAT OAKEN SELLS?

SURE!

ANNA → BANNER!

OAKEN

AND KRISTOFF, YOU GATHER SOME PEOPLE AND TAKE THEM ON A TRIP TO THE POST, OKAY?

EXCITING!

I LIKE IT!

GREAT! LET'S START WORKING!

SO THE HARD WORK BEGINS...

EVERYONE WILL SEE THESE BANNERS.

AND...

INTERESTING!

WHERE'S THIS PLACE?

YOU CAN ASK MY FRIENDS, OVER THERE!

THANKS, PRINCESS ANNA!

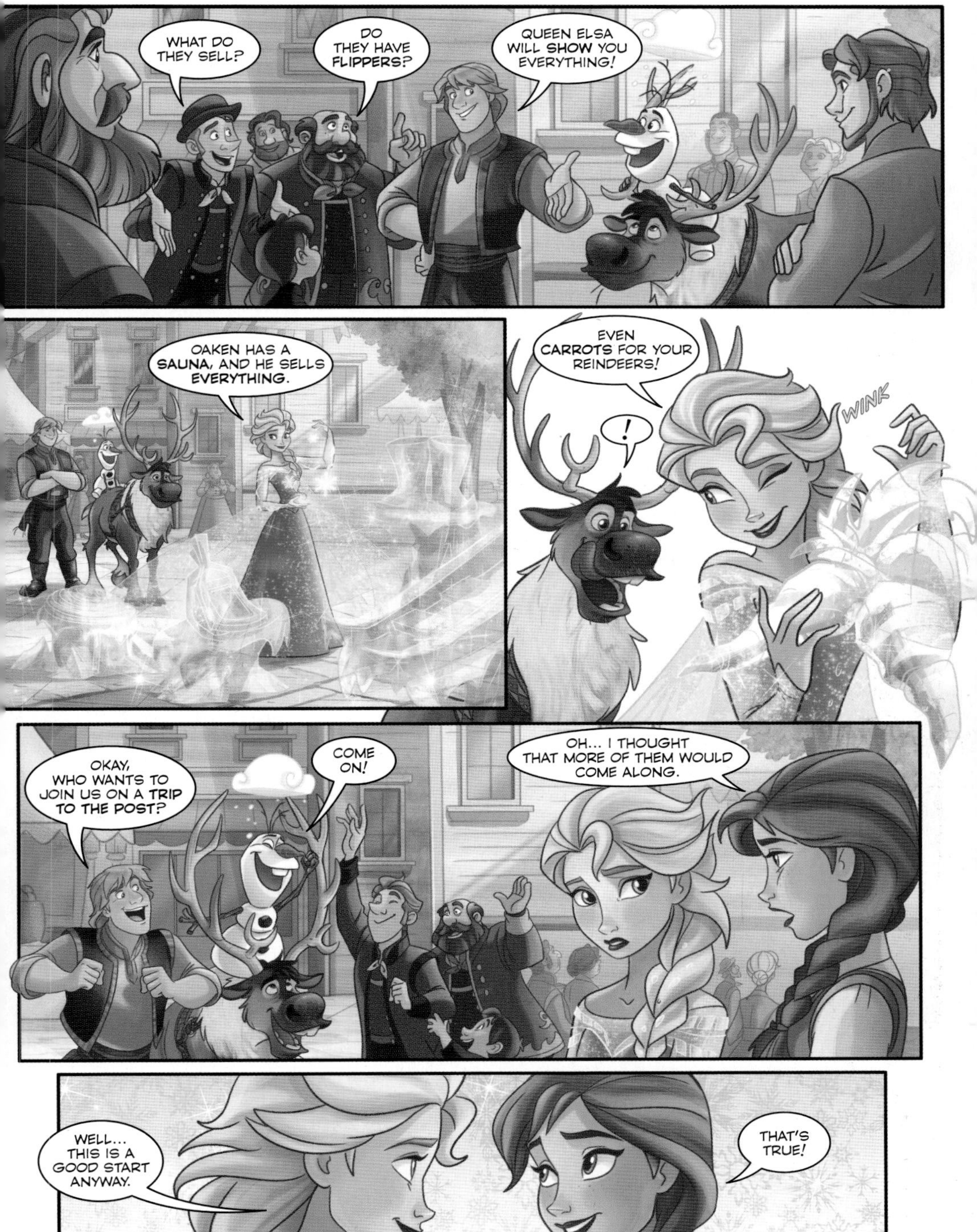
WHAT DO THEY SELL?
DO THEY HAVE FLIPPERS?
QUEEN ELSA WILL SHOW YOU EVERYTHING!
OAKEN HAS A SAUNA, AND HE SELLS EVERYTHING.
EVEN CARROTS FOR YOUR REINDEERS!
!
WINK
OKAY, WHO WANTS TO JOIN US ON A TRIP TO THE POST?
COME ON!
OH... I THOUGHT THAT MORE OF THEM WOULD COME ALONG.
WELL... THIS IS A GOOD START ANYWAY.
THAT'S TRUE!

BUT WHEN THE LITTLE GROUP REACHES THE POST...

YIKES!

INCREDIBLE!

OAKEN WON'T BE LONELY ANYMORE!

LOOKS LIKE ANNA'S SIGNS REALLY WORKED!

AND, INSIDE...

I DON'T KNOW WHAT HAPPENED, BUT I HAVE A LOT OF CUSTOMERS NOW!

I SEE, OAKEN! I SEE!

GREAT PLAN, ANNA! WE REALLY HELPED OAKEN'S BUSINESS.

YES, BUT I THINK HE'LL NEED OUR HELP AGAIN SOON...

THERE ARE TOO MANY CUSTOMERS FOR JUST ONE OAKEN!

WHERE CAN WE FIND ANOTHER OAKEN?

HA HA!

The End

REINDEER GAMES

THE REINDEER RACING CHAMPIONSHIP!

HAS IT STARTED YET?

NO, WE'RE EARLY. THE RACE WON'T START FOR ANOTHER HOUR.

KRISTOFF!

Writer: Georgia Ball; Layouts: Benedetta Barone; Inks: Veronica Di Lorenzo, Paulo Borges, Letizia Algeri; Colors: Ekaterina Maximenko, Manuela Nerolini, Cecilia Giumento, Yanna Chinstova, Nastia Beloushova; Letters: AndWorld Design

YAN, THIS IS QUEEN ELSA, PRINCESS ANNA AND OLAF.

I MET YAN WHEN I HELPED THE REINDEER HERDERS CROSS TO THEIR WINTER GRAZING PASTURES.

IT'S AN HONOR!

YAN HAS BEEN TRAINING ALL YEAR FOR THE RACE!

MY REINDEER, RØREK AND RØNNIK, DO MOST OF THE WORK.

BUT I MADE THE SLED MYSELF!

IT'S LIGHT AND STURDY ENOUGH TO CAPTURE THE LEAD, I THINK.

"TELL YOUR FRIEND HE HAS A NICE SLED!"

"TELL *YOUR* FRIEND HE SHOULD RACE US SOMETIME!"

HA-HA...

I CAN SEE WHY YOU TWO ARE FRIENDS!

WHO IS THAT? HE DOESN'T LOOK HAPPY TO SEE YOU...

THAT'S SNORRI, LAST YEAR'S WINNER. I THINK HE'S HEARD HOW FAST MY RACING TIME HAS BEEN ON OUR PRACTICE RUNS.

I'M KEEPING MY EYE ON HIM...

...SOME OF THE OTHER COMPETITORS SAY HE DOESN'T RACE FAIR.

NEVER MIND HIM, YAN. I KNOW YOU CAN HANDLE ANYTHING.

THE SUN IS GETTING HIGH, SO YOU'LL HAVE TO EXCUSE ME...

...I NEED TO PREPARE THE SLED FOR THE RACE.

WE'LL MEET YOU AT THE STARTING LINE...

"THERE ARE A LOT MORE EVENTS TO SEE."

ONE MORE PLANK SHOULD DO IT...

KER-PASH

FOOLISH RAGCOAT! YOU CAN'T BUILD A TOWER TO THE SUN...

NOT IF I DON'T TRY! IT'S JUST LIKE I ALWAYS SAY...

...NEVER GIVE UP!

"NEVER GIVE UP!" THAT SOUNDS JUST LIKE ANNA...

...RAGCOAT IS REALLY SMART.

YOU CAN LEARN A LOT FROM PUPPETS AND SNOWMEN.

LOOK-- THEY'RE LASSOING PEGS!

WAIT, PEGS CAN'T GET AWAY...

KRISTOFF!

RØREK IS MISSING!

HE WANDERED OFF?

NO... HIS ROPE WAS CUT, AND SOMEONE BRUSHED AWAY HIS TRACKS.

AND THEN A MAN GAVE ME A MESSAGE--HE SAID HE HAD JUST COME FROM MY VILLAGE...

...MY PARENTS NEED ME BACK HOME AT ONCE-- MY FATHER HAS FALLEN ILL. IT SEEMS UNLIKELY SO MANY BAD THINGS COULD HAPPEN AT ONCE, BUT I CAN'T TAKE THE CHANCE.

I MUST GO HOME RIGHT AWAY.

THAT'S TERRIBLE!

YOU WORKED SO HARD ON YOUR SLED THIS YEAR...

...WHAT IF I RACED IT FOR YOU?

I WOULD LIKE TO SEE WHAT MY SLED CAN DO. ARE YOU SURE YOU AND SVEN ARE READY TO RACE?

FOR A FRIEND IN NEED WE'RE ALWAYS READY, RIGHT SVEN?

WE'LL LOOK FOR RØREK, YAN.

THANK YOU! I'LL BE BACK AS SOON AS I CAN. GOOD LUCK, KRISTOFF...

HAVE YOU DONE MUCH RACING BEFORE?

A LITTLE...

I THINK YOU COULD USE A RACING PARTNER!

I THINK YOU'RE RIGHT.

START

SOMEONE LOOKS A LITTLE DISAPPOINTED TO SEE YAN'S SLED.

SNORRI NEEDS TO GET USED TO DISAPPOINTMENT.

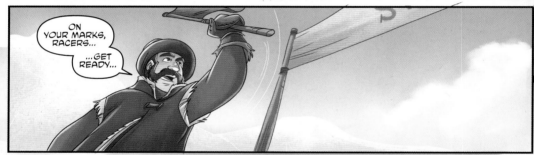

ON YOUR MARKS, RACERS...

...GET READY...

START

GO!

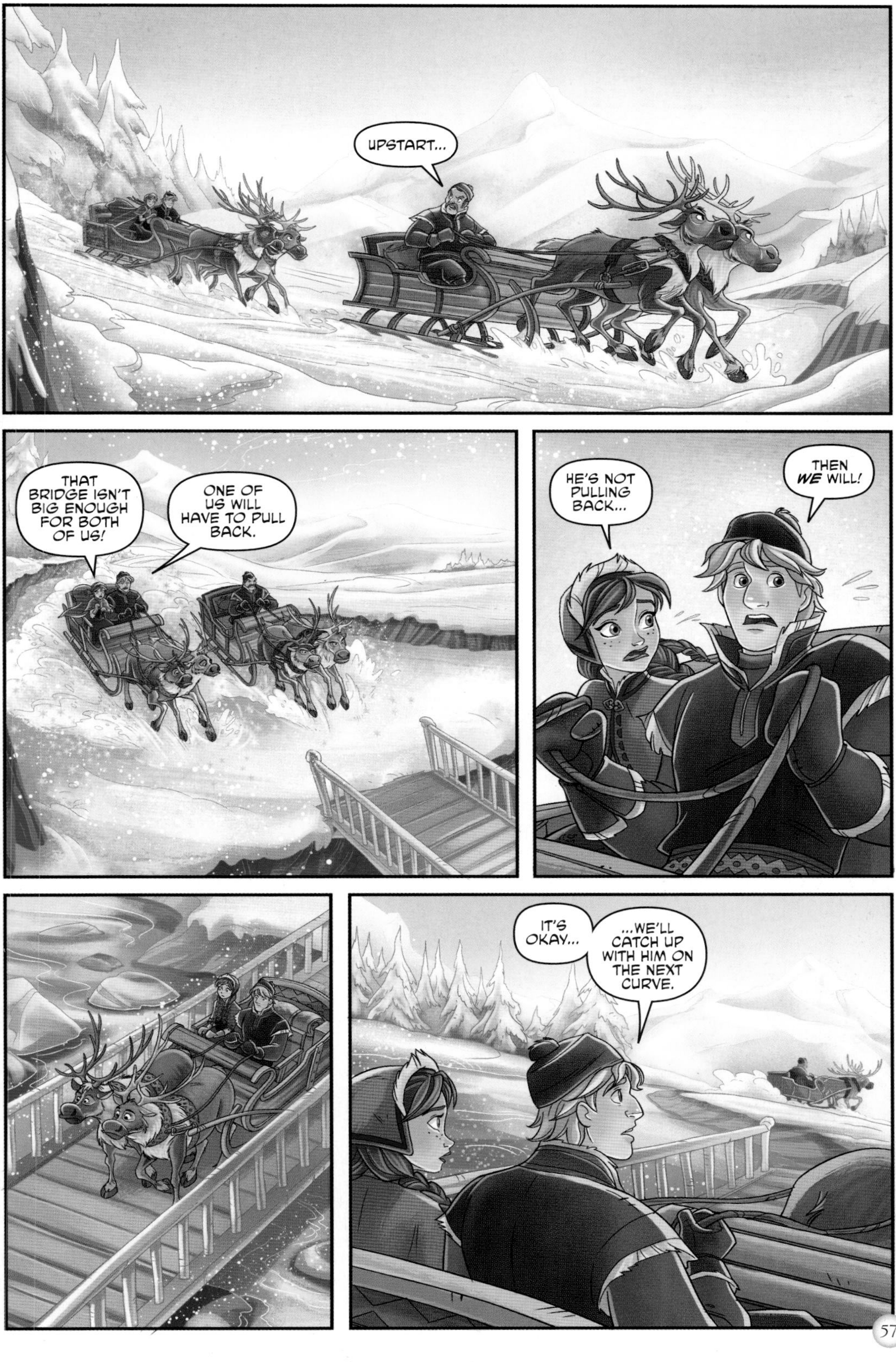
UPSTART...
THAT BRIDGE ISN'T BIG ENOUGH FOR BOTH OF US!
ONE OF US WILL HAVE TO PULL BACK.
HE'S NOT PULLING BACK...
THEN WE WILL!
IT'S OKAY...
...WE'LL CATCH UP WITH HIM ON THE NEXT CURVE.

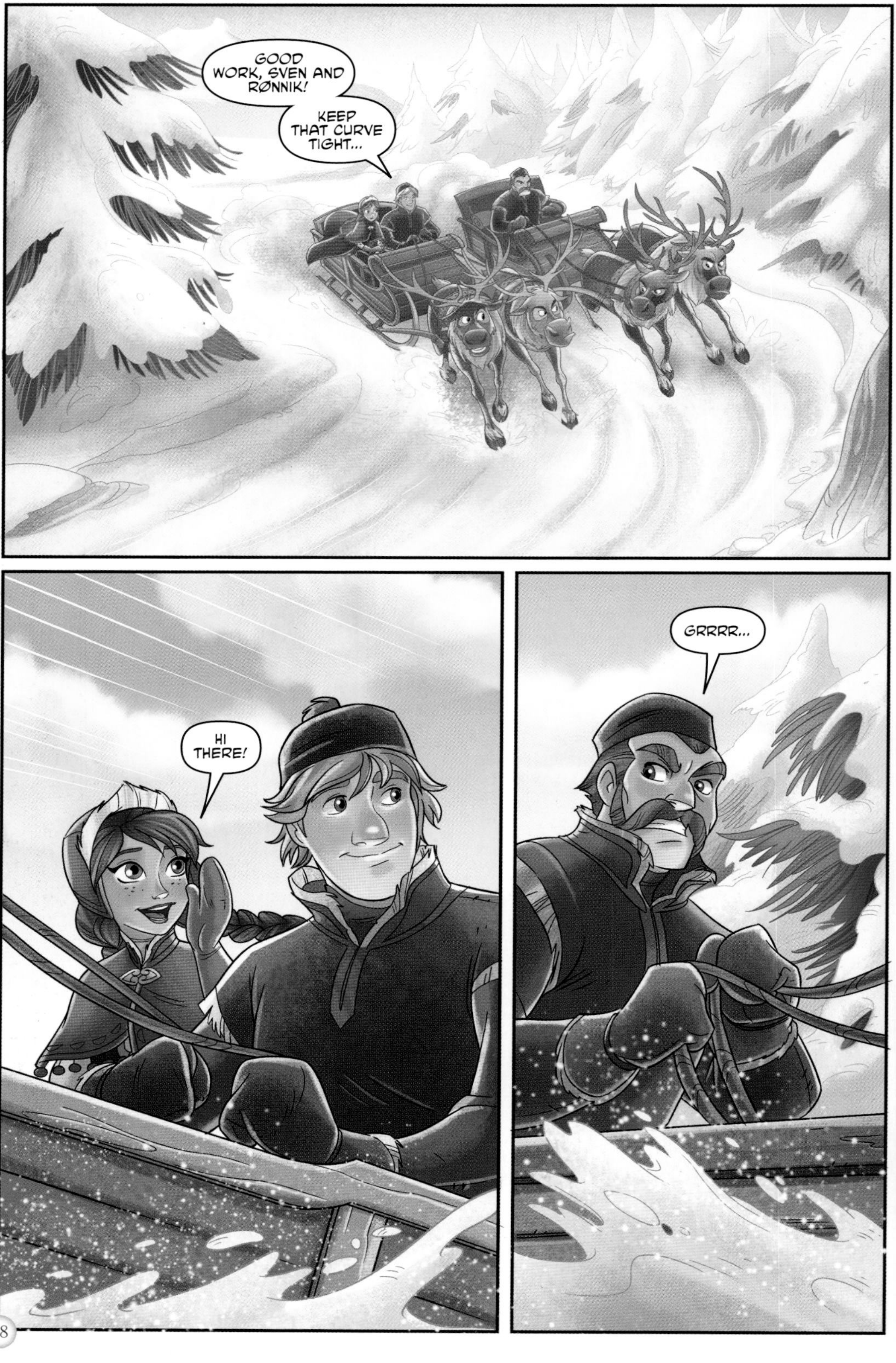
GOOD WORK, SVEN AND RØNNIK!
KEEP THAT CURVE TIGHT...
HI THERE!
GRRRR...

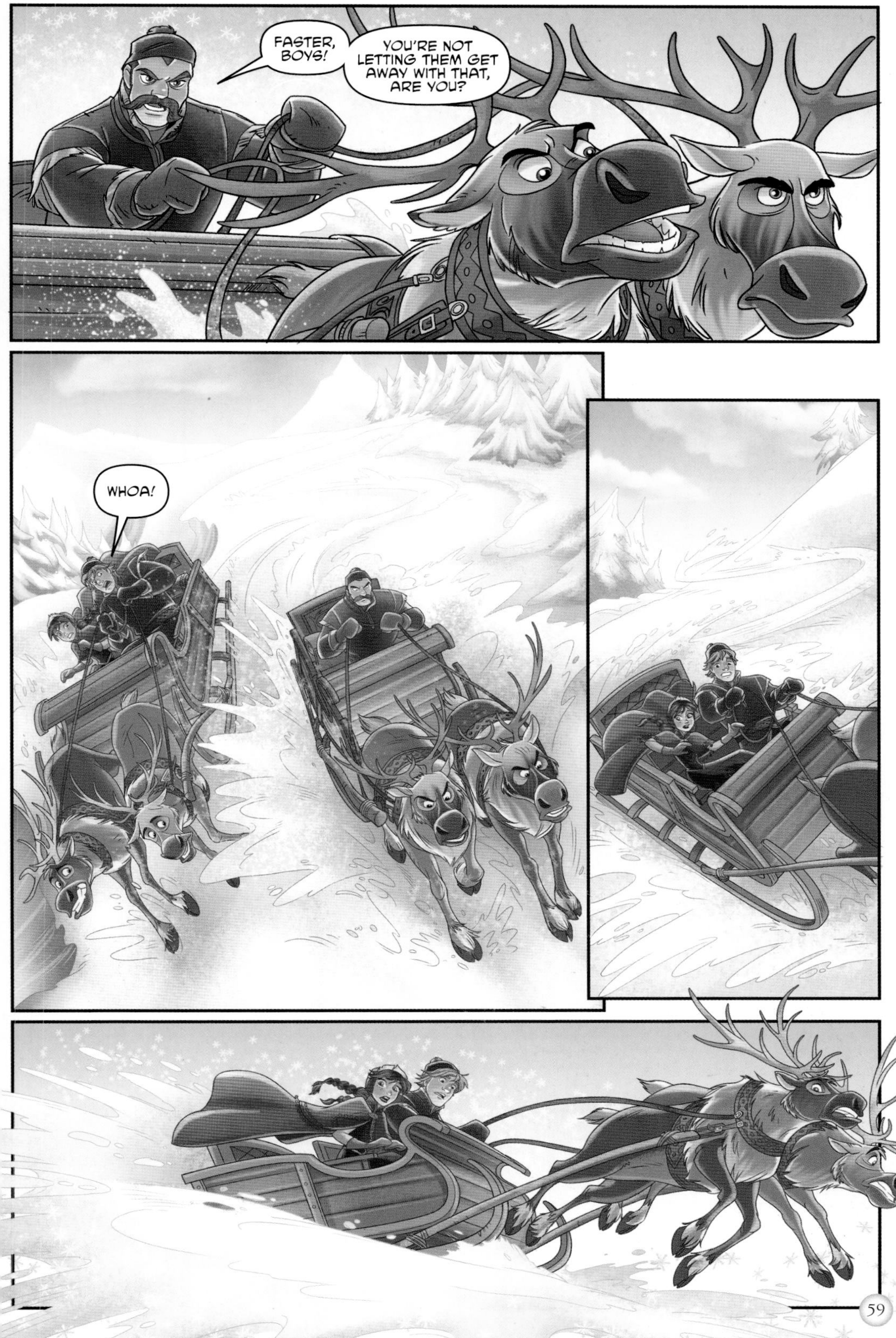
FASTER, BOYS!
YOU'RE NOT LETTING THEM GET AWAY WITH THAT, ARE YOU?
WHOA!

IS EVERYONE OKAY?

I THINK SO, ARE YOU?

YES... THE REST OF THE RACERS ARE PASSING US...

...I GUESS WE'RE OUT.

NO, KRISTOFF! DON'T YOU REMEMBER WHAT RAGCOAT SAID?

"NEVER GIVE UP!"

HEH...

WE'RE NOT DONE YET, ARE WE SVEN?

"WE'RE JUST GETTING STARTED!"

UP WE GO!

PUFF PUFF

YOU DID IT! WE'RE BACK IN THE RACE!

HOW DID--?

CHUNK

AAAIIIEEEE!

SWOOOOSH

WE MADE IT TO THE FINISH...

PUPPETS HAVE GREAT ADVICE!

SECOND PRIZE, CONGRATULATIONS.

MY FATHER WASN'T SICK AFTER ALL...

AND ELSA AND OLAF FOUND RØREK!

WHERE WAS RØREK?

TIED UP BEHIND SNORRI'S SHELTER WITH A BUNCH OF CARROTS.

...THEN THE MESSAGE FROM YOUR VILLAGE WAS A TRICK...

BY ONE OF SNORRI'S FRIENDS, NO DOUBT.

WELL, THIS REALLY BELONGS TO YOU...

...WE WOULD NEVER HAVE WON IT WITHOUT YOUR REINDEER AND YOUR SLED.

I ALREADY TOLD THE JUDGE WHERE WE FOUND RØREK, AND ABOUT THE FALSE EMERGENCY.

I THINK IT WILL BE A LONG TIME BEFORE ANYONE LETS SNORRI RACE AGAIN.

IT'S GETTING LATE...

...WE SHOULD START BACK FOR ARENDELLE.

WHAT AN EXCITING RIDE! I'M SORRY YOU MISSED IT, YAN.

THAT'S ALL RIGHT...

...TOMORROW WE'LL START TRAINING FOR NEXT YEAR!

The End

THE BEST DRINK EVER

WHAT ABOUT A CUP OF THE BEST DRINK EVER?

WOW!

FOR YOU!

IS IT HOT COCOA?

OF COURSE! DON'T YOU LIKE IT?

IT'S TOO HOT FOR TODAY...

BUT I HAVE AN IDEA...

AND...

YUM! I LOVE ICY COCOA ON A SUNNY DAY!

ME, TOO!

Manuscript: Tea Orsi; Layout: Emilio Urbano; Cleanup: Manuela Razzi; Color: Dario Calabria

The End

IS IT TIME YET?

Manuscript: Tea Orsi; Layout: Emilio Urbano;
Cleanup: Nicoletta Baldari; Color: Dario Calabria

THE YUMMIEST COLLECTION EVER

THIS COLLECTION USED TO BELONG TO OUR ANCESTORS!

WHAT IS A COLLECTION, ELSA?

IT'S A GROUP OF SPECIAL OBJECTS, JUST LIKE THESE PLATES!

OOOH!

WHY DON'T WE GET A COLLECTION TOO, SVEN?

!

GREAT IDEA! WHAT WILL YOU COLLECT?

WELL...I... DON'T KNOW!

THINK ABOUT SOMETHING YOU LIKE!

I LIKE SUMMER! BUT WE CAN'T COLLECT SUMMERS...

Manuscript: Tea Orsi; Layout: Alberto Zanon; Cleanup: Nicoletta Baldari; Color: Manuela Nerolini

WHAT ABOUT CARROTS? SVEN LOVES THEM!

THAT'S A GOOD IDEA! YOU CAN GET THEM AT OAKENS!

LATER...

A CHUBBY ONE, A SKINNY ONE, A LONG ONE, A SHORT ONE...

THANKS OAKEN! THIS IS AN AMAZING CARROT COLLECTION!

I CAN'T WAIT TO SHOW IT TO ANNA AND ELSA!

BACK AT THE CASTLE...

COME AND SEE OUR COLLECTION!

HUH?!? WHAT IS GOING ON?

ERM... I THINK YOUR COLLECTION WAS THE PERFECT BREAKFAST FOR SVEN, OLAF!

CHOMP!

The End

THROUGH THE WALL

A SUNNY NEW DAY HAS JUST BEGUN IN ARENDELLE, WHEN...

GOOD MORNING, ELSA!

ARE YOU READY FOR OUR TRIP?

OH, I THINK I AM!

GREAT! WE'LL EXPLORE THE WOODS...

CLACK

UPS!...

AND WE'LL CLIMB THE HIGHEST MOUNTAIN... OOOOOH...

CAREFUL, ANNA!

Manuscript: Tea Orsi; Layout: Alberto Zanon; Cleanup: Miriam Gambino; Color: Patrizia Zangrilli and Manuela Nerolini

WHAT?!

HUH?!

HEY, IT'S WINDY!

LET'S HAVE A LOOK...

THIS LOOKS LIKE A...SECRET DOOR!

WHERE COULD IT GO?

HOW EXCITING!

I THINK YOU ACTIVATED SOMETHING THAT OPENED THE DOOR!

WHAT'S BEHIND THAT DOOR?

I DON'T KNOW...BUT WE'LL FIND OUT!

ANNA AND ELSA RUSH TO TELL KRISTOFF AND SVEN ABOUT THEIR DISCOVERY...

A SECRET DOOR YOU NEVER KNEW ABOUT?

THAT'S RIGHT. WE HAD NO IDEA IT WAS THERE!

COME ON, LET'S GO!

BE CAREFUL, IT'S VERY **DARK**. USE YOUR LANTERN AND WATCH YOUR STEP!

THIS PASSAGE IS STEEP. I WONDER WHERE IT LEADS... MAYBE JUST TO THE CELLAR?

OR SOMEWHERE REALLY SPECIAL!

MAYBE TO THE BEACH!

YOU NEVER KNOW, OLAF!

AT THE END OF THE STAIRS...

BRRR! IT'S FREEZING DOWN HERE!

I THINK THAT WE MIGHT BE UNDERGROUND NOW. LET'S KEEP GOING!

WE ARE COLD, TOO! I HAVE AN IDEA!

"...LET'S WALK ALL CLOSER TO EACH OTHER!"

SO...

NOW... ERM... I'M NOT COLD ANYMORE, BUT I CAN'T MOVE!

UH OH!

WOOSH

THE CEILING IS MADE OF WATER!

NOT EXACTLY, OLAF. I THINK WE ARE UNDER THE CASTLE MOAT!

MANY MORE STEPS LATER...

WE'VE BEEN WALKING FOR AGES!

HOLD ON! I HEAR SOMETHING...

TRRR TOCK TOCK

I THINK SOMEONE IS WALKING JUST ABOVE OUR HEADS!

LOOK!

THAT'S A BRICK DOOR!

IT WON'T BUDGE!

I BET NO ONE HAS OPENED IT FOR CENTURIES!

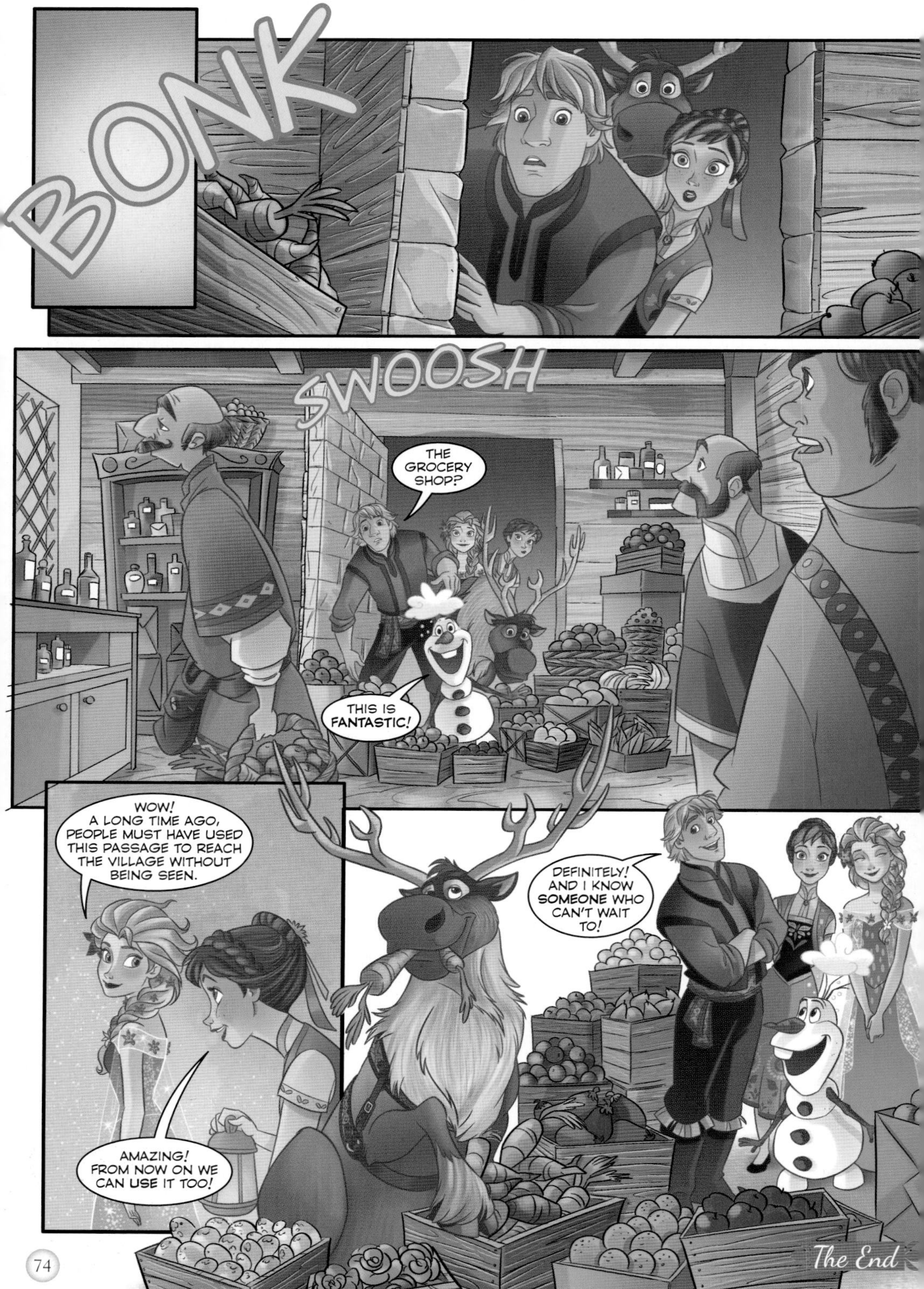
BONK
SWOOSH
THE GROCERY SHOP?
THIS IS FANTASTIC!
WOW! A LONG TIME AGO, PEOPLE MUST HAVE USED THIS PASSAGE TO REACH THE VILLAGE WITHOUT BEING SEEN.
AMAZING! FROM NOW ON WE CAN USE IT TOO!
DEFINITELY! AND I KNOW SOMEONE WHO CAN'T WAIT TO!
The End

SNOWY SNACKS

ELSA AND GERDA ARE MAKING COOKIES FOR THE VILLAGE KIDS, WHEN...

I LOVE BAKING! CAN I HELP YOU?

I CAN PUT THE COOKIES INTO THE OVEN!

ERM...IT'S A BIT TOO HOT FOR YOU, OLAF...

BUT WE CAN MAKE ANOTHER KIND OF TREAT WITHOUT USING IT!

A LITTLE BIT OF SNOW, AND...

WOW! MAKING ICE CREAM IS SO MUCH FUN!

SUGAR

AND YOU ARE THE BEST HELPER EVER, OLAF!

Manuscript: Tea Orsi; Layout: Alberto Zanon; Cleanup: Miriam Gambino; Color: Dario Calabria

The End

A Good Friend

HELLO, BUDDY!

?!

HEY, WHAT ARE YOU DOING?!?

THIS IS MY NOSE, NOT YOUR FOOD!

UMPF!

NO NO NO!

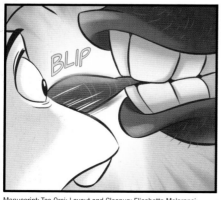

BLIP

OH! THANKS MY FRIEND. YOU FIXED IT!

!

Manuscript: Tea Orsi; Layout and Cleanup: Elisabetta Melaranci; Color: Dario Calabria

The End

An Early Bird

ARE YOU READY FOR OUR TRIP?

I COULDN'T BE MORE READY, ELSA!

I LOVE TRIPS!

WE WILL DO SO MANY THINGS TOGETHER! WE WILL SEE THE FJORDS AND FISH, SWIM...

WE'LL MAKE IT A PERFECT TRIP, YES. BUT DON'T FORGET THAT WE HAVE TO LEAVE EARLY IN THE MORNING.

anuscript: Alessandro Ferrari; Layout: Gianluca Barone; Cleanup: Michela Farace; Color: Dario Calabria

THIS IS SO BEAUTIFUL! I WANT TO SHOW IT TO ANNA!

ANNA?

GOOD MORNING, ANNA!

OLAF?! WAIT... I'M AWAKE!

ANNA?

THANK YOU, OLAF. LUCKY FOR ME, YOU DON'T SLEEP. I COULD NEVER... ZZZ

YES! I CAN DO THIS! I CAN DO THIS!

FIRST THING, COMB MY HAIR... WOW, THIS MAY TAKE LONGER THAN EXPECTED!

NOW WE TRY NOT TO WAKE EVERYONE UP YET.

WHERE ARE WE GOING?

TO PREPARE THE LUNCHES FOR THE TRIP!

OH, THE TRIP!

OLAF, ISN'T THAT TOO BIG?

NOT FOR SVEN! HE LOVES CARROTS!

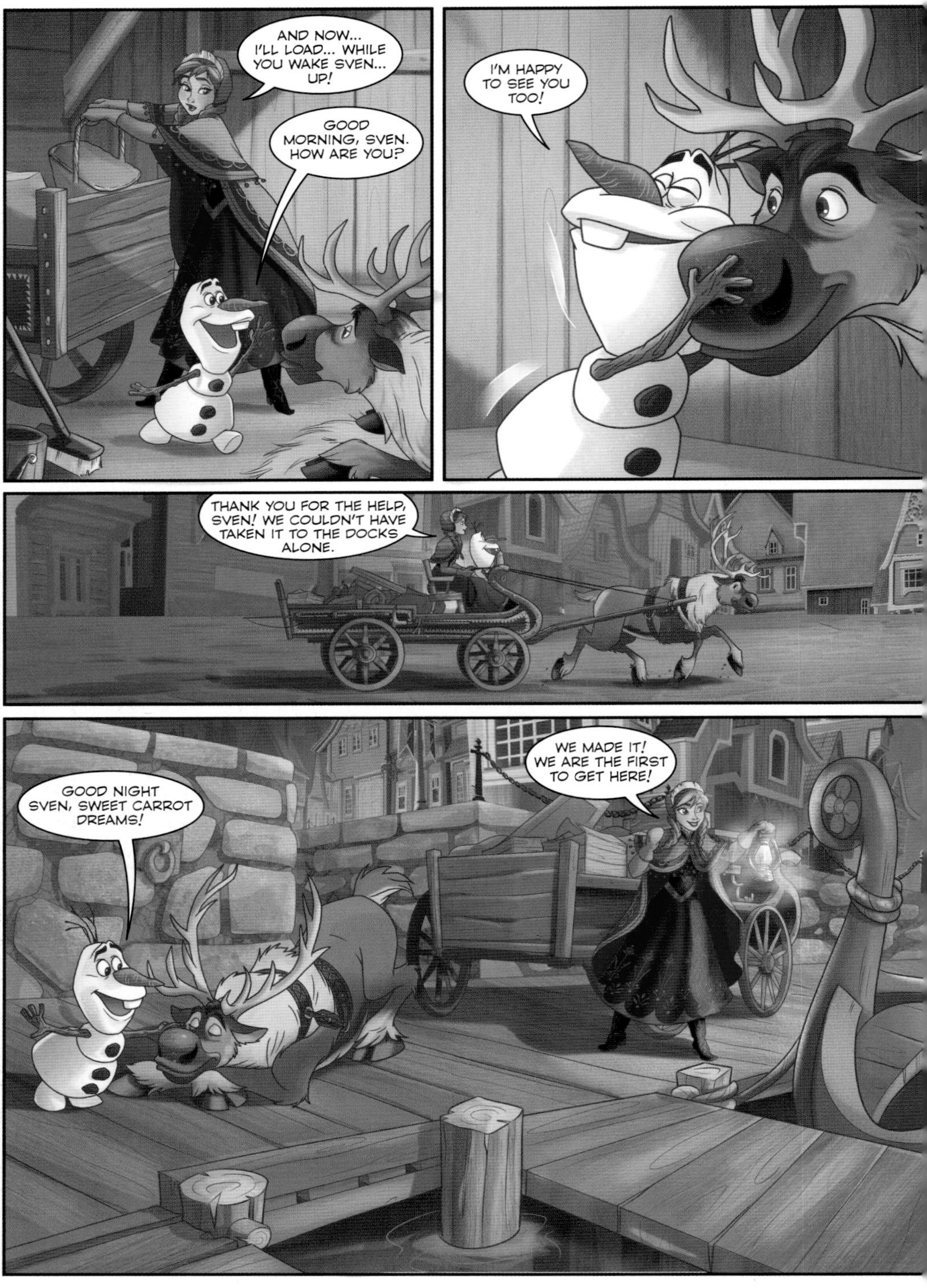
AND NOW... I'LL LOAD... WHILE YOU WAKE SVEN... UP!
GOOD MORNING, SVEN. HOW ARE YOU?
I'M HAPPY TO SEE YOU TOO!
THANK YOU FOR THE HELP, SVEN! WE COULDN'T HAVE TAKEN IT TO THE DOCKS ALONE.
GOOD NIGHT SVEN, SWEET CARROT DREAMS!
WE MADE IT! WE ARE THE FIRST TO GET HERE!

I'VE NEVER WOKEN UP THIS EARLY BEFORE.

IT FEELS AMAZING... YAWN!

IT'S LIKE... LIKE... YAAAWN!

LATER...

... AND SO YOU AND SVEN HELPED HER GET HERE BEFORE ANYONE ELSE!

ZZZ

THIS TRIP IS REALLY IMPORTANT TO HER, ISN'T IT?

SHOULD WE WAKE HER?

I'LL DO IT! I'M GREAT AT WAKING PEOPLE UP!

ZZZ

I COULD BECOME EVERYONE'S WAKE-UP FRIEND!

HAHAHAH!

HAHAHAH!

The End

SO MANY COLORS

TONIGHT I'LL MAKE A **PAINTING** OF THE NORTHERN LIGHTS!

GOOD IDEA, I'LL CARRY YOUR **PAINT BOX!**

THANKS, BUT I WON'T NEED THE WHOLE BOX. I'LL JUST TAKE A FEW... **BLUE** AND **BROWN**...

... AND SOME **WHITE**. MAYBE **ORANGE** AND **GREEN** TOO!

ALSO **RED** AND **YELLOW** AND A TOUCH OF **LAVENDER**...

OOOOOH! CAN I BORROW THAT **BOX** TO CARRY THEM IN?

OH, SURE!

Manuscript: Tea Orsi; Layout: Manuela Razzi; Cleanup: Marino Gentile; Ink: Michela Frare; Color: Stefania Santi

The End

CARROT NOSES

Manuscript: Tea Orsi; Layout: Alberto Zanon; Cleanup: Marino Gentile; Color: MichelAngela World

The End

The Flangendorfer Secret

IT'S A GLORIOUS MORNING IN ARENDELLE...

ELSA, AREN'T YOU EXCITED? TODAY IS THE DAY OF FLANGENDORFERS!

FLANGEN... WHAT?

THE FLANGENDORFERS!

I'VE NEVER HEARD OF A "FLANGENDORFER."

YOU MEAN YOU'VE NEVER TASTED ONE? I HEAR THEY'RE THE MOST DELICIOUS DESSERT IN ALL OF ARENDELLE! AND WE'RE GOING TO DISCOVER THEIR SECRET RECIPE.

BUT... I HAVE WORK TO DO.

DISCOVERING THE BIG SECRETS OF YOUR KINGDOM IS WORK.

OKAY, ONE FLANGENDORFER WON'T HURT!

Original story by Erica David; Manuscript adaptation by Chantal Pericoli; Layout: Gianluca Barone; Cleanup: Letizia Algeri; Color: Dario Calabria

IT'S AMAZING. THE SHOP ITSELF LOOKS GOOD ENOUGH TO EAT!

Florian's Bakery

AND WHAT'S INSIDE LOOKS EVEN BETTER.

AHEM!

!!!

MY QUEEN, ALLOW ME TO INTRODUCE MYSELF...

CHEF FLORIAN, AT YOUR SERVICE.

!!!

NICE TO MEET YOU!

MAY I PRESENT TO YOU THE FINEST DESSERT IN ALL OF ARENDELLE!

SNAP

WOW!

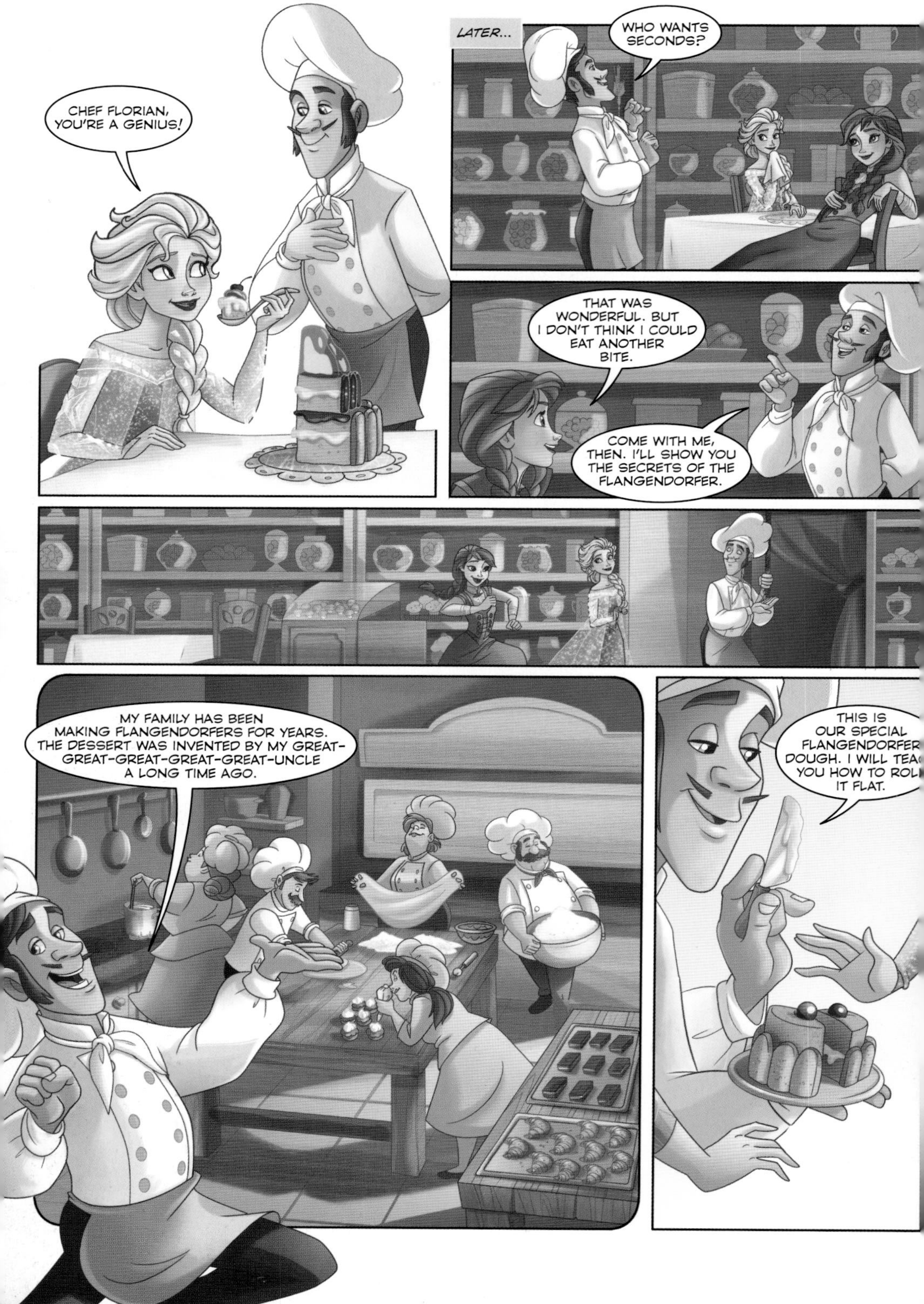
CHEF FLORIAN, YOU'RE A GENIUS!
LATER...
WHO WANTS SECONDS?
THAT WAS WONDERFUL. BUT I DON'T THINK I COULD EAT ANOTHER BITE.
COME WITH ME, THEN. I'LL SHOW YOU THE SECRETS OF THE FLANGENDORFER.
MY FAMILY HAS BEEN MAKING FLANGENDORFERS FOR YEARS. THE DESSERT WAS INVENTED BY MY GREAT-GREAT-GREAT-GREAT-GREAT-UNCLE A LONG TIME AGO.
THIS IS OUR SPECIAL FLANGENDORFER DOUGH. I WILL TEAC YOU HOW TO ROL IT FLAT.

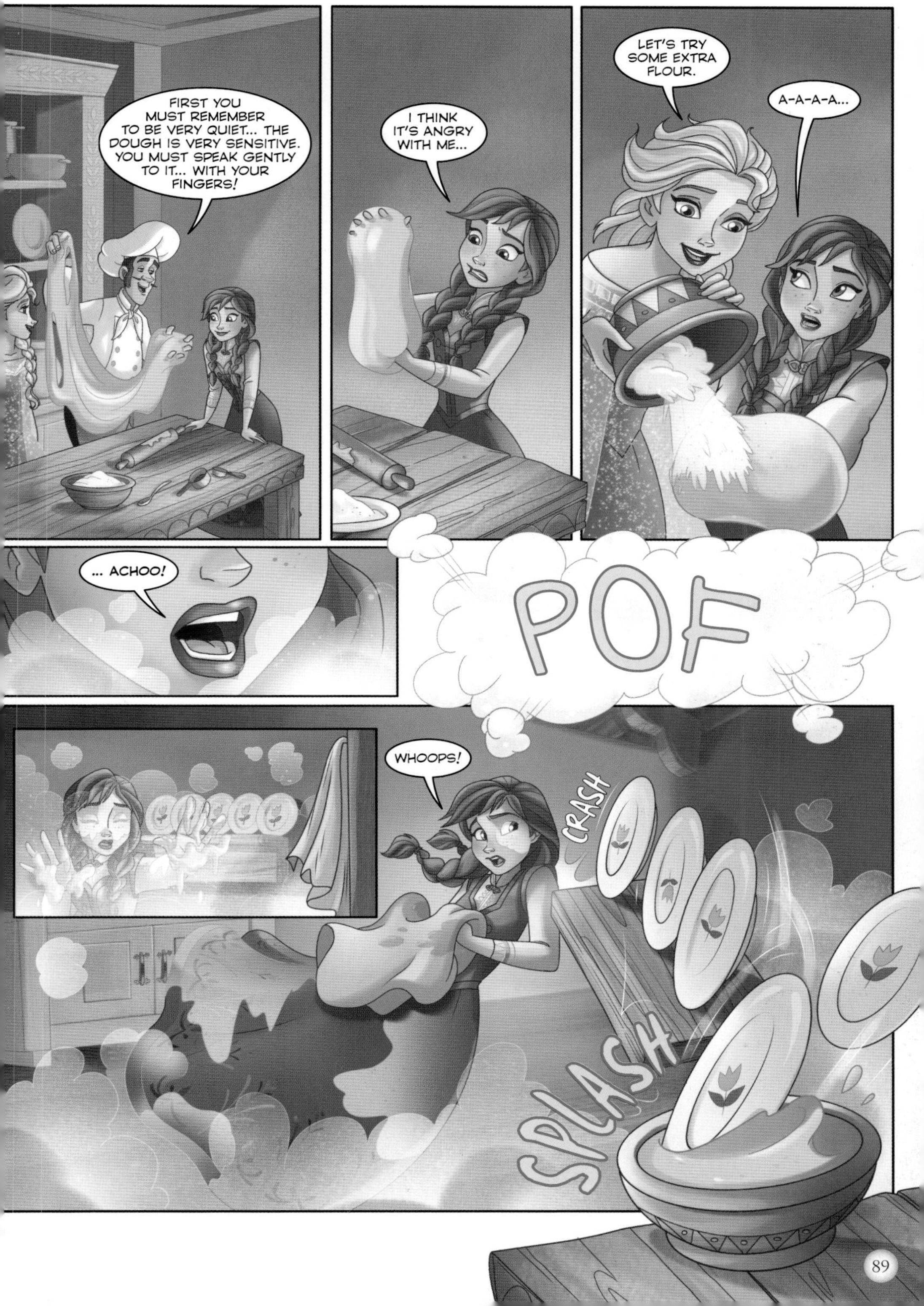
FIRST YOU MUST REMEMBER TO BE VERY QUIET... THE DOUGH IS VERY SENSITIVE. YOU MUST SPEAK GENTLY TO IT... WITH YOUR FINGERS!
I THINK IT'S ANGRY WITH ME...
LET'S TRY SOME EXTRA FLOUR.
A-A-A-A...
... ACHOO!
POF
WHOOPS!
CRASH
SPLASH

HUMPH!

SORRY, ANNA. THIS BIG MESS IS ALL MY FAULT.

MMMPH!

I THINK WE SHOULD APOLOGIZE TO FLORIAN.

MMMPH!

I KNOW YOU'RE UPSET, BUT WON'T YOU AT LEAST SAY SOMETHING?

MMMPH!

OH, YOUR LIPS! THEY'RE SEALED SHUT FROM THAT BATTER!

WELL, AT LEAST YOU WON'T REVEAL CHEF FLORIAN'S SECRET RECIPE! HAHAHA!

The End

Special Break

IT'S A BEAUTIFUL SPRING DAY, BUT...

SIGH...

HUH?!?

ELSA, WHAT'S WRONG? YOU LOOK A BIT SAD!

WELL, I LOVE THIS WARM WEATHER, BUT...

BUT YOU MISS THE FREEZING WINTER, DON'T YOU?!

EXACTLY!

I THINK IT'S TIME FOR A RELAXING SNOW-AND-ICE BREAK!

LATER, AT THE ICE PALACE...

WELL, MAYBE THIS IS NOT EXACTLY THE RELAXING BREAK I HAD IN MIND...

WE CAN ALWAYS CALL IT SNOW-AND-PLAY BREAK! HA HA!

Manuscript: Tea Orsi; Layout: Emilio Urbano; Cleanup: Nicoletta Baldari; Color: Dario Calabria

The End

A Great Landing

HELLO BANNISTER, MY FAVORITE SPOT IN THE CASTLE!

IF I SLIDE REALLY FAST I CAN LAND RIGHT IN FRONT OF THE DOOR...

... OR MAYBE RIGHT ON THE FLOWER VASE! I HOPE I WON'T BREAK IT THIS TIME...

KRISTOFF?!?

WHAT--?

DEFINITELY THE SOFTEST PLACE I'VE EVER LANDED!

?!?

Manuscript: Tea Orsi; Layout: Manuela Razzi; Cleanup: Manuela Razzi; Color: Maria Claudia Di Genova

 The End

STRAIGHT INTO ACTION

Manuscript: Tea Orsi; Layout: Alberto Zanon; Cleanup: Rosa La Barbera; Color: Manuela Nerolini

HUH?!? THEY FELL **ASLEEP**!

ZZZZ

OH NO, THEY WILL **MISS** THE LIGHTS!

SWOOOSH

MAYBE WE SHOULD **WAKE** THEM UP.

YES, BUT WE NEED TO FIND A **GENTLE** WAY TO DO IT!

ERM... YOU KNOW...

HMMM?

... I THINK SVEN IS TAKING CARE OF THAT!

WE ARE SO HIGH UP!

LOOK AT THE LIGHTS!

LET'S GO!

GOOD JOB, SVEN! THAT WAS A GREAT IDEA!

YOU ARE BETTER THAN AN ALARM CLOCK, BUDDY!

The End

A Map from the Past

ELSA IS AWAY ON AN OFFICIAL VISIT, AND ANNA IS LOOKING FOR BOOKS ABOUT TRAVELING THAT THEY CAN READ TOGETHER WHEN SHE'S BACK...

"WINTER ADVENTURES," "A NORTHERN JOURNEY".

THAT'S A HARD CHOICE!

I'LL TAKE THIS ONE... COUGH, COUGH!

ACHOO

POFF!

HUH?!?

POCK

Manuscript: Tea Orsi; Layout: Marino Gentile; Clean: Sara Storino and Michela Frare; Color: MichelAngela World

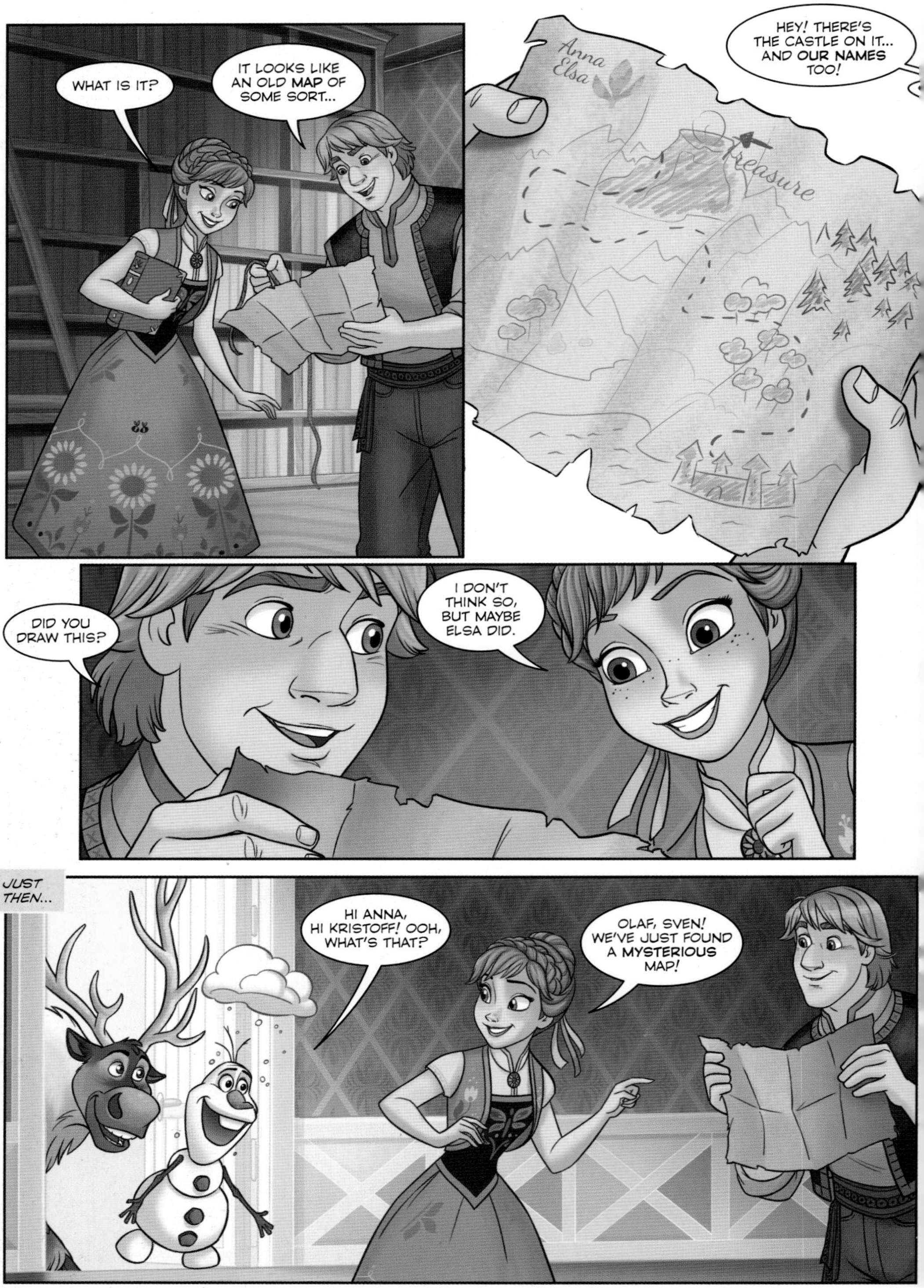
WHAT IS IT?
IT LOOKS LIKE AN OLD MAP OF SOME SORT...
Anna
Elsa
Treasure
HEY! THERE'S THE CASTLE ON IT... AND OUR NAMES TOO!
DID YOU DRAW THIS?
I DON'T THINK SO, BUT MAYBE ELSA DID.
JUST THEN...
HI ANNA, HI KRISTOFF! OOH, WHAT'S THAT?
OLAF, SVEN! WE'VE JUST FOUND A MYSTERIOUS MAP!

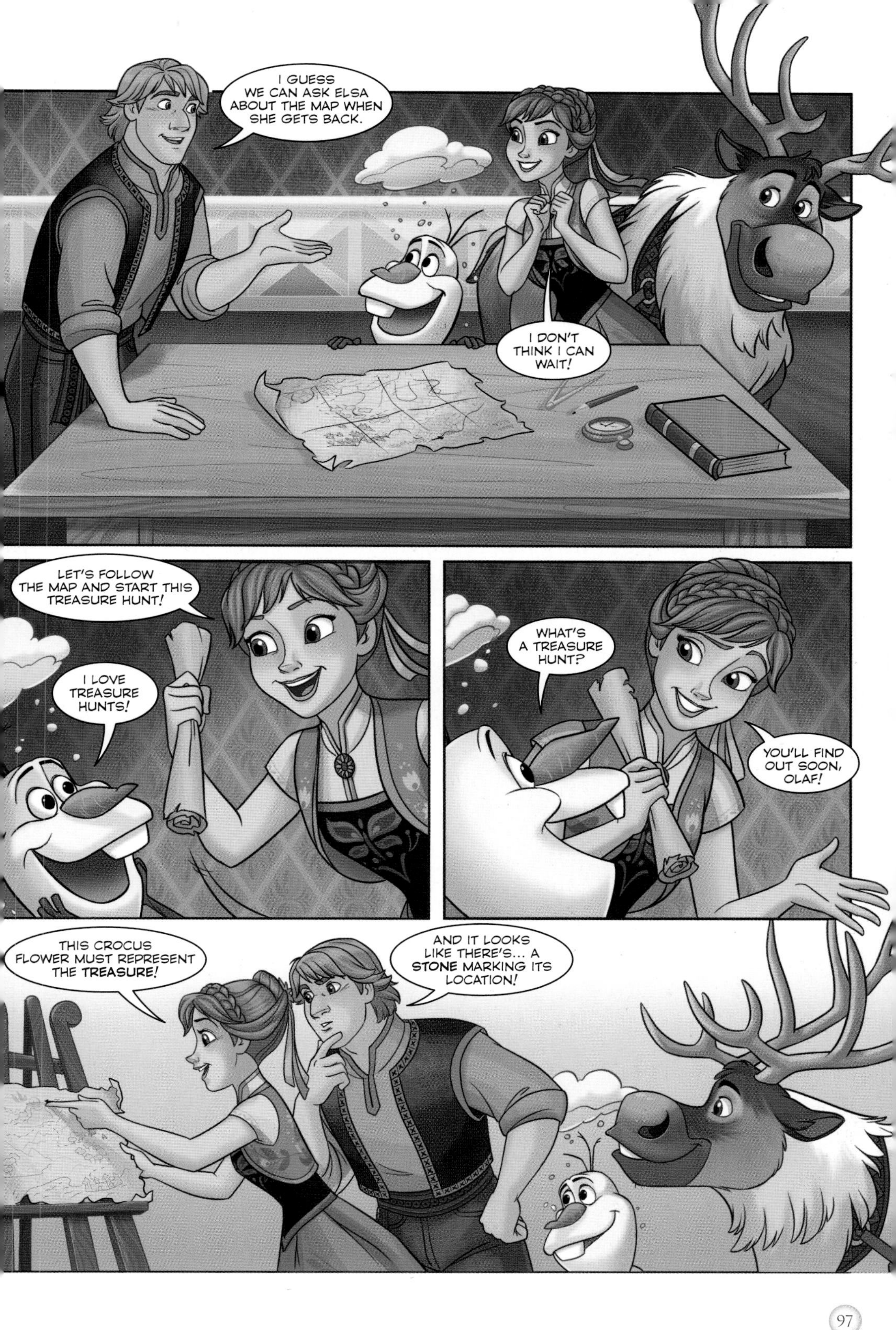
I GUESS WE CAN ASK ELSA ABOUT THE MAP WHEN SHE GETS BACK.
I DON'T THINK I CAN WAIT!
LET'S FOLLOW THE MAP AND START THIS TREASURE HUNT!
I LOVE TREASURE HUNTS!
WHAT'S A TREASURE HUNT?
YOU'LL FIND OUT SOON, OLAF!
THIS CROCUS FLOWER MUST REPRESENT THE **TREASURE**!
AND IT LOOKS LIKE THERE'S... A **STONE** MARKING ITS LOCATION!

SOON...

HEY, KRISTOFF...
ARE WE HEADING TO
ÆLDSTE PEAK?

LOOKS
LIKE IT!

THERE'S A
PASS THROUGH THE
MOUNTAIN THAT MATCHES
THE DRAWING ON
THE MAP.

"I LOVE TAKING THIS
PATH IN WINTER..."

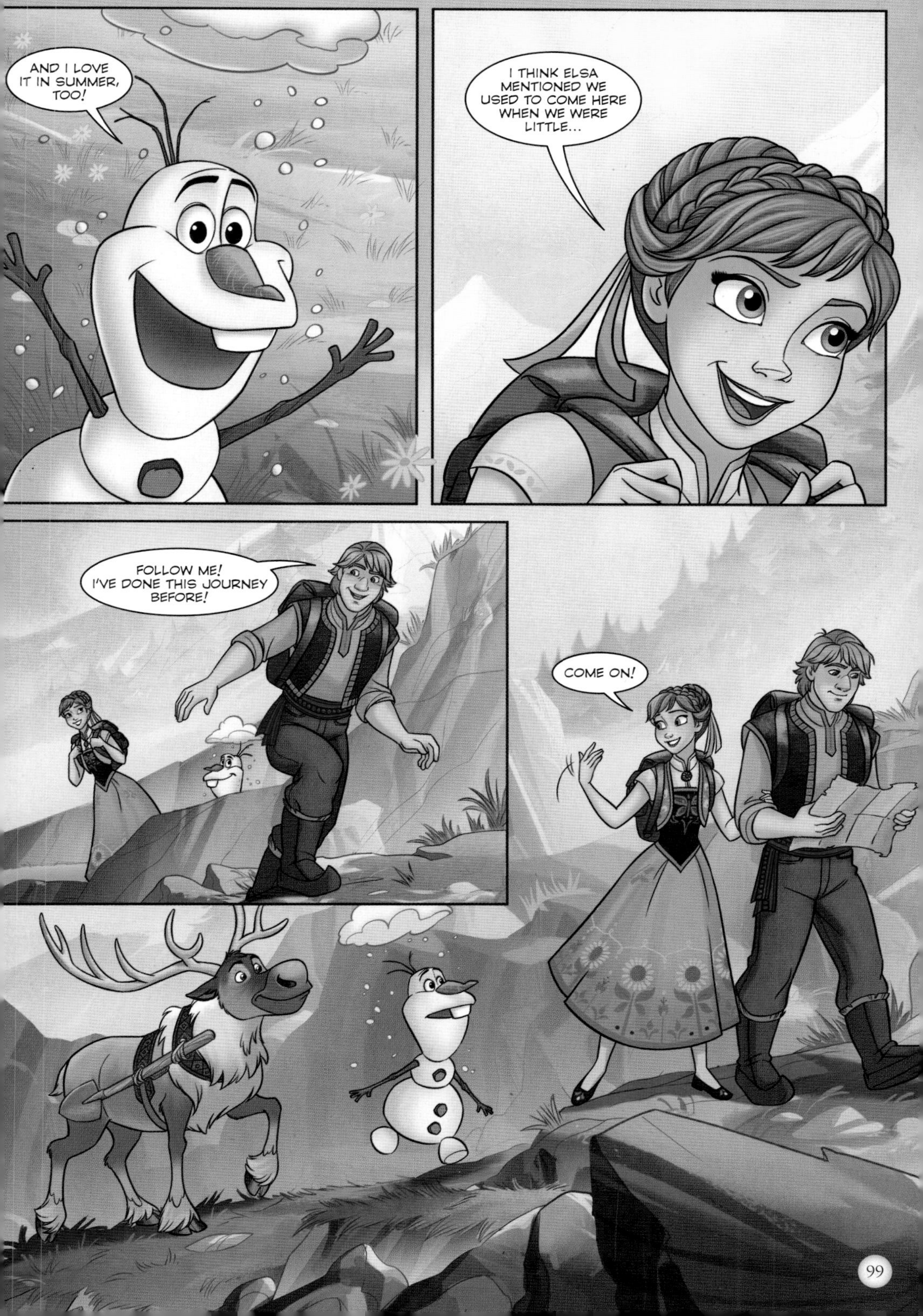
AND I LOVE IT IN SUMMER, TOO!
I THINK ELSA MENTIONED WE USED TO COME HERE WHEN WE WERE LITTLE...
FOLLOW ME! I'VE DONE THIS JOURNEY BEFORE!
COME ON!

FINALLY...

HERE WE ARE! THIS IS THE CLEARING PICTURED ON THE MAP!

ACCORDING TO THE MAP, THERE SHOULD BE A... STONE...

YES, BUT I CAN'T SEE ANY...

I'M SURE IT'S HERE SOMEWHERE.

WHERE?

I DON'T KNOW! THE MAP WAS DRAWN MANY YEARS AGO. MAYBE SOMETHING CHANGED...

WILL OUR FRIENDS FIND THE MYSTERIOUS TREASURE? LET'S DISCOVER IT IN PART 2 OF THIS EXCITING ADVENTURE!

End Of Part 1

A Map from the Past

Part 2

EVERYONE STARTS SEARCHING FOR THE MYSTERIOUS STONE...

LET'S LOOK EVERYWHERE!

MAYBE IT'S COVERED BY MOSS!

BUT SOMEONE GETS A LITTLE BIT DISTRACTED...

OOHHH! YOUR WINGS ARE BEAUTIFUL!

DO YOU WANT TO BE MY FRIEND?

anuscript: Tea Orsi; Layout: Marino Gentile; Clean: Sara Storino and Michela Frare; Color: MichelAngela World

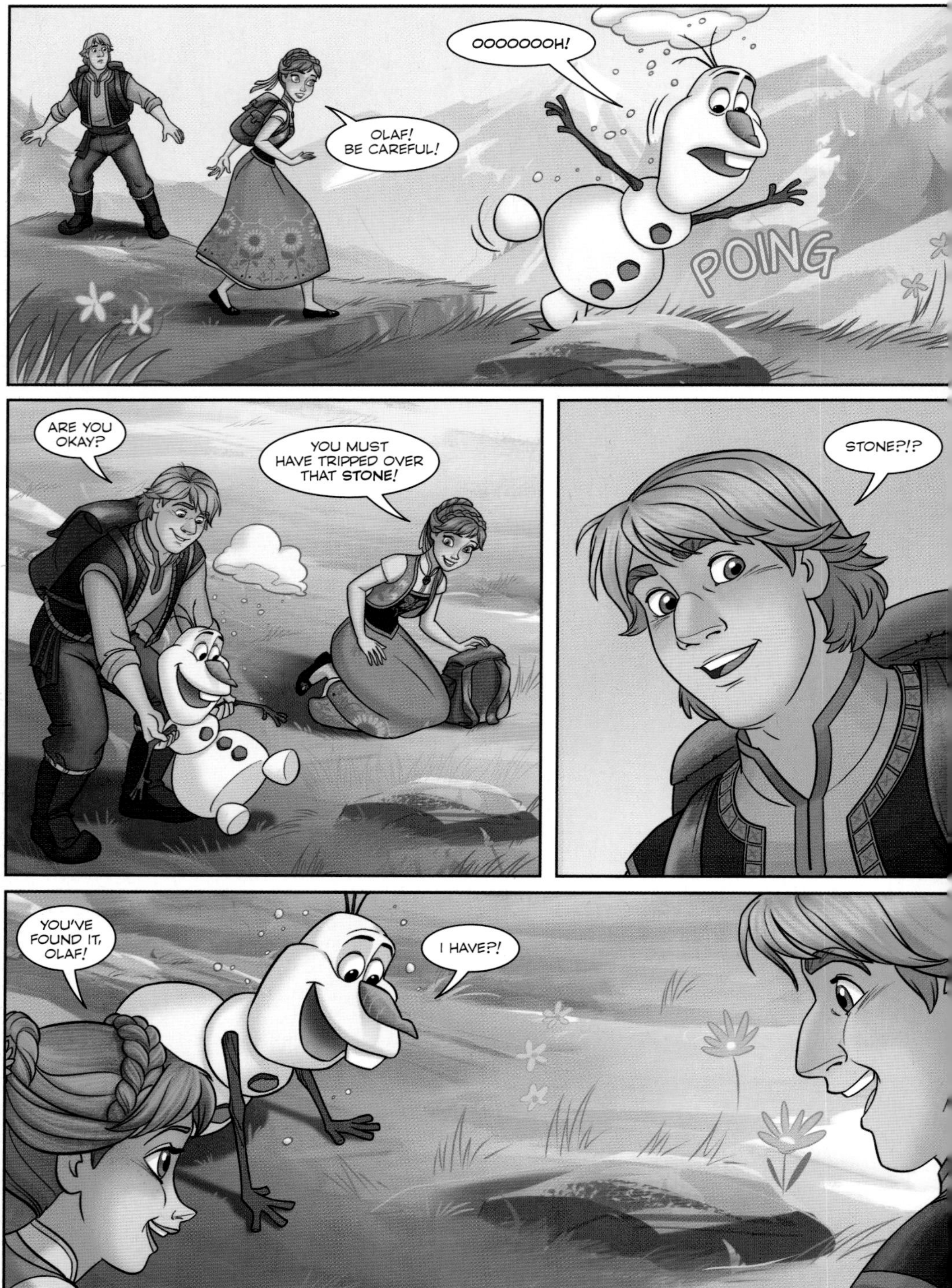
OLAF! BE CAREFUL!
OOOOOOOH!
POING
ARE YOU OKAY?
YOU MUST HAVE TRIPPED OVER THAT STONE!
STONE?!?
YOU'VE FOUND IT, OLAF!
I HAVE?!

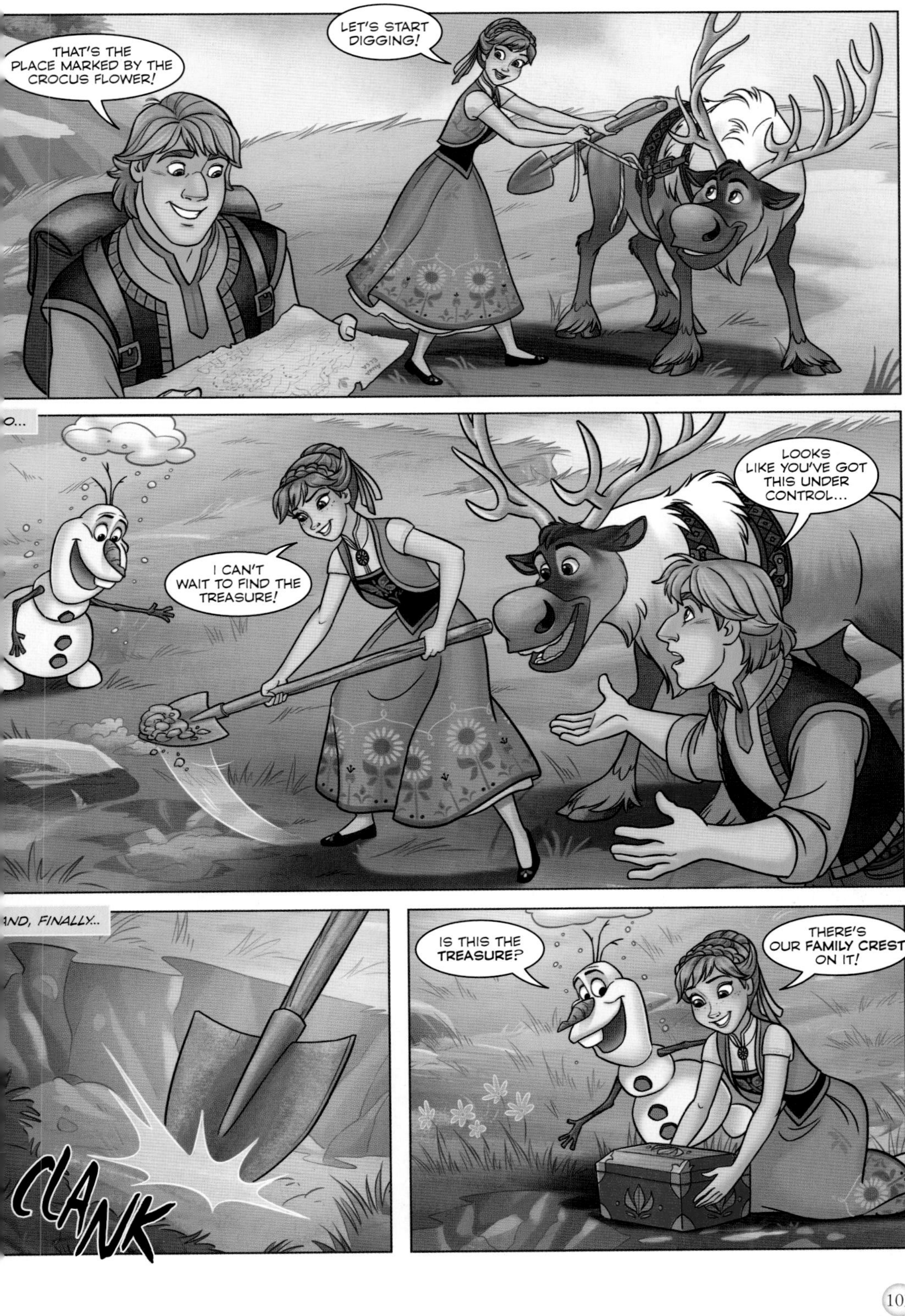

THAT'S THE PLACE MARKED BY THE CROCUS FLOWER!
LET'S START DIGGING!
O...
I CAN'T WAIT TO FIND THE TREASURE!
LOOKS LIKE YOU'VE GOT THIS UNDER CONTROL...
ND, FINALLY...
CLANK
IS THIS THE **TREASURE**?
THERE'S OUR **FAMILY CREST** ON IT!

COME ON, LET'S OPEN IT!

OH NO! THE BOX IS LOCKED.

DON'T WORRY, WE'LL FIGURE OUT A WAY TO GET IT OPEN!

MAYBE THE KEY IS BACK AT THE CASTLE SOMEWHERE...

LET'S GO TAKE A LOOK!

BACK HOME, OUR FRIENDS FIND ELSA BACK FROM HER JOURNEY AND...

ANNA?!? WHERE DID YOU FIND THAT... BOX?!?

DO YOU KNOW WHAT'S IN IT?

NOW I WANT TO KNOW EVERYTHING. PLEASE!

I'M SURE YOU REMEMBER THAT YOU LOVED PIRATE STORIES WHEN WE WERE LITTLE...

"SO MOM AND I BURIED THE BOX AND MADE THE MAP...

ANNA WILL HAVE SO MUCH FUN!

"WE WERE PLANNING A DAY FOR THE TREASURE HUNT, BUT THEN YOU AND I HAD TO SEPARATE..."

SO IT WAS THERE ALL THAT TIME?!? NOW I'M EVEN MORE CURIOUS TO SEE WHAT'S INSIDE IT!

YOU'RE LUCKY! I'VE ALWAYS KEPT THE KEY IN MY ROOM...

BUT I COULDN'T REMEMBER WHERE WE HID YOUR TREASURE!

AND, WHEN ELSA AND ANNA OPEN THE BOX...

THESE WERE JUST LITTLE GIFTS MOM AND I MADE FOR YOU, ANNA!

I LOVE THEM, AND THE LONG WAIT MADE THEM EVEN MORE SPECIAL!

CAN YOU DRAW ANOTHER MAP FOR US, ELSA?

SURE, BUT THIS TIME WE WON'T WAIT SO LONG BEFORE GOING ON OUR TREASURE HUNT.

LET'S GET STARTED RIGHT AWAY!

The End

FOLLOW THE RHYTHM!

IT'S A FUN DAY AT THE ICE PALACE...

THE SNOWGIES ARE GREAT LITTLE DANCERS!

THEY REALLY LOVE KRISTOFF'S MUSIC.

POING

POING

POING

POING

PHEW! THAT WAS A LOT OF **STRUMMING**. TIME FOR A **BREAK**!

!!!

BE CAREFUL, BUDDIES. LUTES ARE MEANT TO BE PLAYED, NOT PLAYED ON!

I THINK THEY'RE **TRYING** TO PLAY IT, BUT...

I HAVE AN IDEA!

Script: Tea Orsi; Layout: Benedetta Barone; Clean: Benedetta Barone; Color: MichelAngela World

LATER...

BHUMP
BHUMP BHUMP
BHUMP

ISN'T IT GREAT?! NOW THE SNOWGIES CAN PLAY WITH KRISTOFF!

WELL, DRUMS ARE JUST PERFECT FOR THEM.

BUT MARSHMALLOW DOESN'T LOOK TOO HAPPY ABOUT THE NOISE...

THE MUSIC MUST BE TOO LOUD FOR HIS EARS.

NO PROBLEM. I'VE GOT JUST THE THING!

WELL DONE, ELSA! NOW ALL OF US CAN ENJOY THE SNOWGIES' MUSIC!

BHUMP
BHUMP
BHUMP
BHUMP

The End

STINGING FRIEND

cript: Tea Orsi; Layout: Benedetta Barone; Cleanup: Letizia Algeri; Color: Silvano Scolari

AND HERE'S THE LAST...

SHOO! GO AWAY!

BZZZZZZZ

PHEW, THAT WAS CLOSE!

BZZZZZZZ

BZZZZZ

I LIKE RUNNING WITH YOU!

HEY! DOOON—

THUMP

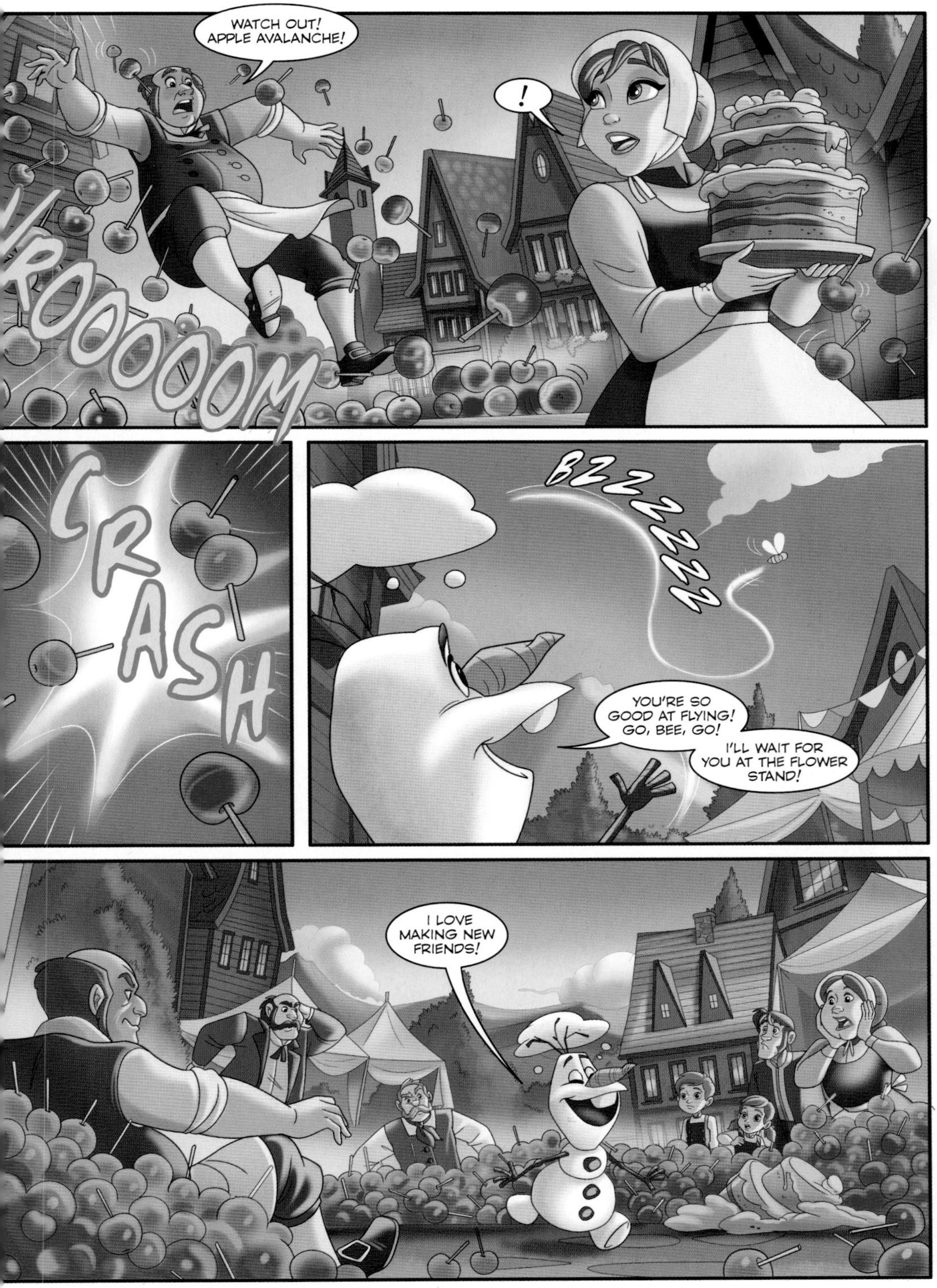
WATCH OUT! APPLE AVALANCHE!
!
VROOOOOM
CRASH
BZZZZZZZ
YOU'RE SO GOOD AT FLYING! GO, BEE, GO!
I'LL WAIT FOR YOU AT THE FLOWER STAND!
I LOVE MAKING NEW FRIENDS!

LATER...

I WONDER WHERE MY NEW PAL WENT?

OH, OLAF. I'M SURE THE BUMBLEBEE WILL COME BUZZING BACK.

THANK YOU, SVEN!

YOU'RE BACK!

BZZZZZZZ

BZZZZZZ

EVERYONE, MEET MY NEW HONEY FESTIVAL PAL!

The End

THE SPRING REINDEER

IT'S ARENDELLE'S NATIONAL DAY AND EVERYONE IS GETTING READY TO CELEBRATE...

THE CASTLE WILL LOOK BEAUTIFUL!

JUST LIKE QUEEN ELSA!

YES, AND PRINCESS ANNA, TOO...

THEIR DRESSES ARE LOVELY.

A FEW MOMENTS LATER...

AHHH!

SVEN! WHERE ARE YOU?

?!?

WHAT HAPPENED TO YOUR ANTLERS?

OOPS...

TEE HEE! I'VE NEVER SEEN SUCH AN ELEGANT REINDEER IN MY WHOLE LIFE!

Manuscript: Tea Orsi; Layout: Manuela Razzi; Cleanup: Nicoletta Baldari; Paint: Dario Calabria

The End

THE MISSING PIECE

ANNA AND KRISTOFF ARE PUTTING TOGETHER A PUZZLE...

THIS IS THE LAST PIECE!

ARE YOU SURE?

YOU'RE RIGHT! THERE'S ONE STILL MISSING...

WHERE COULD IT BE?

HEY, DO YOU LIKE MY NEW BUTTON?

GASP!

I LOVE IT!

I WON'T TELL HIM!

NOR WILL I.

Manuscript: Tea Orsi; Layout and Cleanup: Nicoletta Baldari; Color: Dario Calabria

The End

BACK HOME

ANNA AND ELSA ARE BACK FROM A SHORT JOURNEY...

ANNA! ELSA! **WELCOME BAAAACK!**

WE MISSED YOU!

HELLO, OLAF!

HEEEEELP!

WHO'S SCREAMING?!

THAT FISHERMAN'S IN TROUBLE!

WHAT HAPPENED, SIR?

MY BOAT CRASHED AGAINST A ROCK!

THERE'S A HOLE IN THE HULL!

SWOOSH

QUICK! LET'S REACH HIM!

SWISH

Manuscript: Tea Orsi; Layout: Alberto Zanon; Cleanup: Miriam Gambino; Color: Stefania Santi

A BIT OF MAGIC, AND...

FINALLY...

TOO MUCH CLIMBING

ANNA, ELSA AND KRISTOFF ARE GOING HIKING AND CLIMBING...

ARE YOU SURE YOU DON'T WANT TO COME WITH US, OLAF?

YES! KAI AND GERDA ARE MAKING COOKIES FOR YOU AND I WANT TO HELP!

SVEN AND I WILL LEND THEM AN ARM AND A HOOF!

!

MY ARM IS READY! WHAT ABOUT YOURS, SVEN?

GRÖN MOUNT IS NOT FAR! WE'LL BE BACK SOON!

MAKE A LOT OF COOKIES! WE'LL BE REALLY HUNGRY WHEN WE COME BACK!

OKAY! HAVE FUN!

Manuscript: Tea Orsi; Layout: Alberto Zanon; Cleanup: Letizia Algeri; Color: MichelAngela World

AFTER A NICE HIKE OUR FRIENDS REACH GRÖN MOUNT, BUT...

UHM...MAYBE WE DIDN'T CHOOSE THE BEST PEAK...

YOU'RE RIGHT! WE CAN'T DO MUCH ROCK CLIMBING HERE!

WHY DON'T WE GO TO STEN PEAK, INSTEAD?

YES, IT WILL BE MORE FUN!

AND...

HERE WE ARE!

I CAN'T WAIT TO START CLIMBING!

OKAY, LET'S GET READY THEN...

KRISTOOOOF! COME ON!

HUH?!? THAT WAS QUICK!

HURRY UP! WE'RE WAITING FOR YOU!

MEANWHILE, AT THE CASTLE...

I CAN'T WAIT TO START!

NO, QUEEN ELSA IS NOT HERE AT THE MOMENT!

WHAT IS HAPPENING?

THESE GENTLEMEN NEED TO TALK TO QUEEN ELSA!

IT'S REALLY URGENT!

YES! THIS MAN'S SHEEP WANT TO STEAL MY PASTURE!

NO, YOU WANT TO STEAL MINE!

NO WAY!

WE WILL FIGURE IT OUT!

SVEN AND I CAN GO GET ELSA! SHE'S NOT THAT FAR!

THAT WOULD BE REALLY NICE OF YOU, OLAF!

SOON, AT GRÖN MOUNT...

ELSAAA! ANNAAA! KRISTOOOOF!

?!

THEY CAN'T HEAR US! LET'S CLIMB UP AND LOOK FOR THEM!

IN THE MEANTIME, ON THE TOP OF STEN PEAK...

WOW, THAT WAS GREAT!

YES! AND CLIMBING DOWN WILL BE FUN TOO!

BY THE WAY, I THINK IT'S TIME TO GO BACK HOME NOW!

BUT OLAF AND SVEN ARE SOMEWHERE ELSE...

WHERE HAVE THEY GONE?!?

?

HEY! WHAT ABOUT TRYING TO CLIMB GRÖN MOUNT NOW TOO?

MAYBE ANOTHER DAY, ANNA!

HEY, SVEN! WHY DID YOU STOP?

OLAF?!?

OH! THERE YOU ARE!

WHAT ARE YOU DOING UP THERE?

I THINK THEY GOT STUCK ON THAT LEDGE!

I GUESS WE'RE GOING TO CLIMB GRÖN MOUNT AFTER ALL...

DON'T MOVE!

WE'RE COMING!

PUT YOUR HOOF HERE, SVEN!

BE CAREFUL NOT TO SLIP!

WE ARE CLIMBING DOWN ALL TOGETHER!

EVERYONE GETS BACK TO THE GROUND SAFELY AND, AFTER SOME EXPLANATIONS...

YOU'LL SEE, ELSA! THOSE SHEPHERDS LOOKED REALLY UPSET!

DON'T WORRY! I'M READY!

BUT...

GOOD EVENING, YOUR MAJESTIES! WE APOLOGIZE FOR INTERRUPTING YOUR HIKE!

BUT WHILE WAITING FOR YOU, WE DECIDED TO SHARE THE SAME PASTURE!

OH, THAT'S GREAT!

TOMORROW WE ARE TAKING OUR FLOCKS TO GRÖN MOUNT!

WOULD YOU DO US THE HONOR TO GO WITH US? WE KNOW YOU ALL LOVE CLIMBING!

The End

Up or Down?

Script: Tea Orsi; Layout: Benedetta Barone; Cleanup: Letizia Algeri and Sara Storino; Color: MichelAngela World

IF THE BARK IS FACING UP, THE WOOD KEEPS DRY.

NO WAY, IT KEEPS **DRIER** WHEN THE BARK IS FACING DOWN!

WHAT'S HAPPENING?

CAN WE JOIN IN THEIR GAME?

THEY ARE NOT PLAYING, OLAF. EACH OF THEM WANTS TO STACK THE FIREWOOD IN A DIFFERENT WAY.

I'M AFRAID THEY WILL NEVER FIND A COMPROMISE...

OF COURSE WE WON'T! AND I WON'T TALK TO HIM ANYMORE!

COME ON, YOU ARE GOOD FRIENDS! THERE'S NO NEED TO BE SO UPSET.

LET'S TAKE A REST AND HAVE A GLASS OF LEMONADE. I'M SURE EVERYTHING WILL BE ALL RIGHT!

THANK YOU, PRINCESS ANNA!

COME, SVEN! LET'S HELP THEM FIND A SOLUTION!

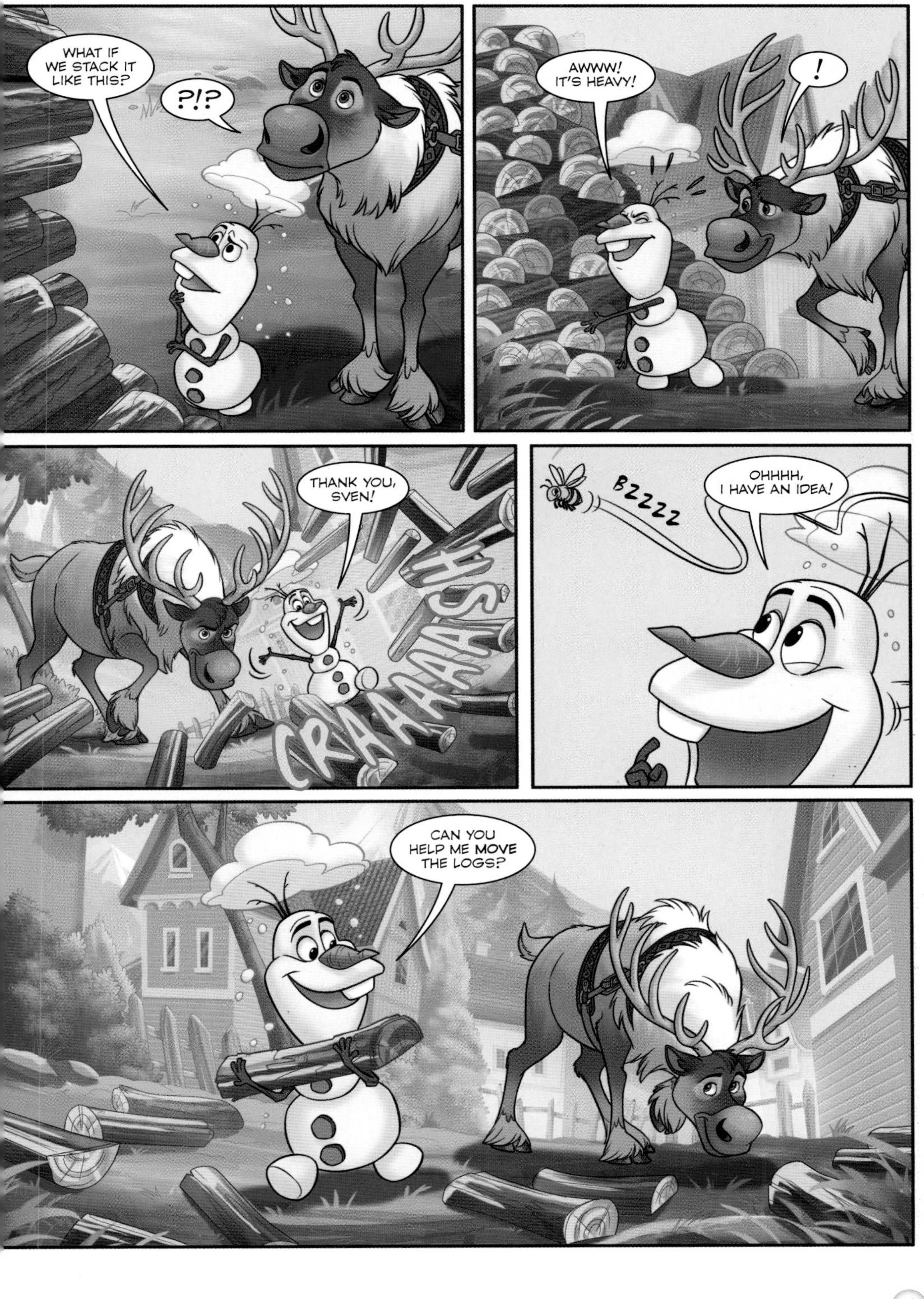
WHAT IF WE STACK IT LIKE THIS?
?!?
AWWW! IT'S HEAVY!
!
THANK YOU, SVEN!
CRAAAAASH
BZZZZ
OHHHH, I HAVE AN IDEA!
CAN YOU HELP ME MOVE THE LOGS?

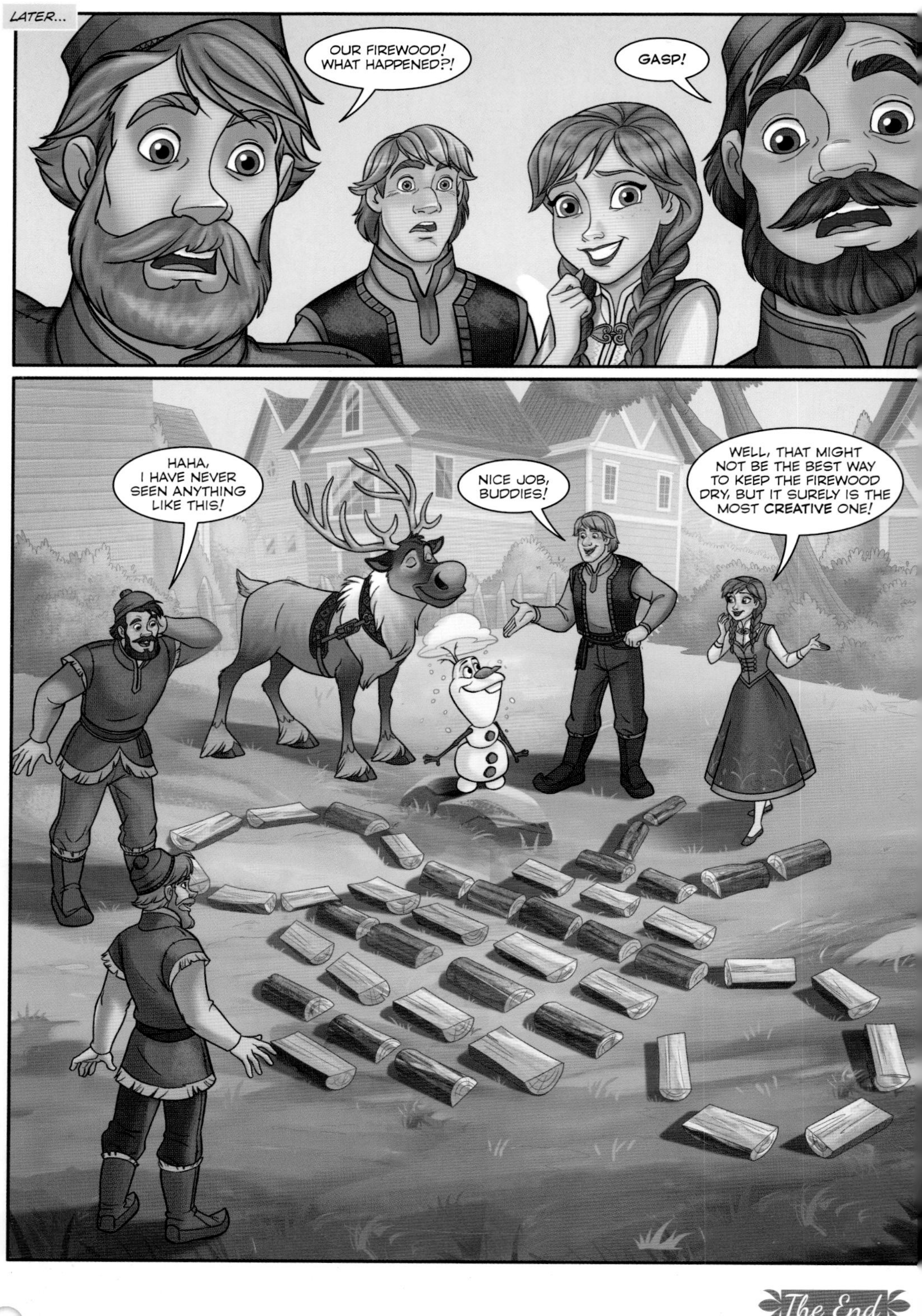
LATER...
OUR FIREWOOD! WHAT HAPPENED?!
GASP!
HAHA, I HAVE NEVER SEEN ANYTHING LIKE THIS!
NICE JOB, BUDDIES!
WELL, THAT MIGHT NOT BE THE BEST WAY TO KEEP THE FIREWOOD DRY, BUT IT SURELY IS THE MOST **CREATIVE** ONE!

The End

Royal Skating Day

ARENDELLE CASTLE: A VERY SPECIAL DAY IS COMING UP...

A LITTLE HIGHER...

A BIT MORE...

YES! WELL DONE! THANK YOU, GUYS!

YOU'RE WELCOME, ANNA!

!?

GOOD MORNING, ANNA! WHAT'S THAT BANNER FOR?

DON'T YOU REMEMBER, ELSA? I'M COORDINATING OUR CELEBRATION... THE ROYAL SKATING DAY IS TOMORROW!

TOMORROW? OH NO!

Manuscript: Alessandro Ferrari; Layout: Elisabetta Melaranci; Cleanup: Arianna Rea, Federica Salfo; Ink: Michela Frare, Cristina Stella; Color: Dario Calabria

I FORGOT ABOUT IT!

NO PROBLEM, SISTER. I'VE TAKEN CARE OF EVERYTHING!

THAT'S GREAT... BUT I HAVE AN IMPORTANT MEETING TOMORROW!

ALL THE DIGNITARIES FROM THE BORDERING COUNTRIES ARE COMING TO ARENDELLE!

!

WE CAN'T HAVE ALL THE ROOMS OF THE CASTLE DECORATED AND AVAILABLE FOR THE PARTY!

I KNOW...

WE MUST FIND A SOLUTION!

WE CAN'T CANCEL THE CELEBRATION, IT'S TOO LATE!

I HAVE ALREADY ARRANGED TEN SKATING CONTESTS, TWO PARTIES, TWO CONCERTS, SIX SNOWBALL FIGHTS, NINE SKATING LESSONS AND, OF COURSE, TONS OF CHOCOLATE!

WE NEED ANOTHER PALACE!

YES! YOU ARE RIGHT!

BUT WE DON'T HAVE ONE...

SHOULD WE HELP THEM?

I DON'T KNOW HOW.

WHAT DO YOU THINK, SVEN?

GREAT IDEA!

?

OLAF TELLS SVEN'S IDEA TO ELSA AND ANNA AND...

THAT'S PERFECT! OLAF, SVEN... THANK YOU SO MUCH!

NOW WE JUST HAVE TO FIND A WAY TO TAKE ALL THE GUESTS UP THERE...

I CAN DO THAT! I'LL ARRANGE SLEDS!

GREAT! YOU HAVE EVERYTHING PLANNED. I'LL TAKE CARE OF THE COUNCIL OF THE DIGNITARIES HERE.

THE FOLLOWING DAY...

... ALL THE GUESTS ARRIVE IN FRONT OF THE MOST WONDERFUL PLACE THEY'VE EVER SEEN...

... *THE ROYAL SKATING PALACE!*

I LOVE THIS PLACE!

ME TOO!

DO YOU THINK THEY'RE ALL ENJOYING THEMSELVES?

EVERYBODY LOVES IT, ANNA!

FASTER, MISTER KRISTOFF!

FASTER, MISTER SVEN!

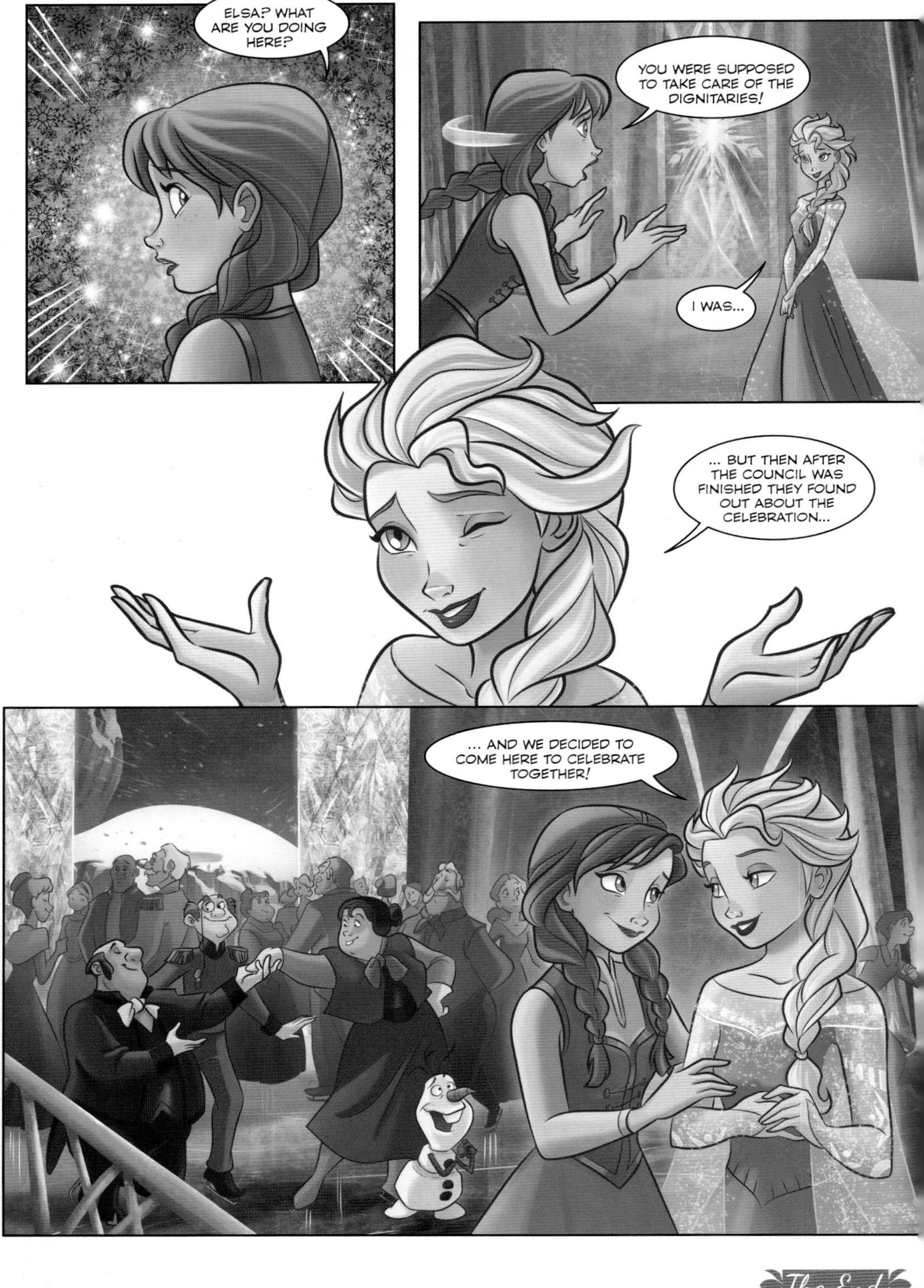
ELSA? WHAT ARE YOU DOING HERE?
YOU WERE SUPPOSED TO TAKE CARE OF THE DIGNITARIES!
I WAS...
... BUT THEN AFTER THE COUNCIL WAS FINISHED THEY FOUND OUT ABOUT THE CELEBRATION...
... AND WE DECIDED TO COME HERE TO CELEBRATE TOGETHER!

The End

A N-Ice Reminder

KRISTOFF AND SVEN ARE TRAVELING TO THE NORTH MOUNTAIN FOR A FEW DAYS...

WE'LL BE BACK SOON!

TAKE CARE OF YOURSELVES!

I MISS THEM ALREADY!

ME TOO, OLAF!

ANNA, OLAF! COME AND SEE!

YOU ALWAYS KNOW HOW TO CHEER US UP, ELSA!

I LOVE THEM!

IT IS NOT THE SAME AS HAVING THE **REAL ONES** HERE, BUT IT'LL BE A NICE REMINDER UNTIL THEY GET BACK!

Manuscript: Tea Orsi; Layout: Emilio Urbano; Cleanup: Rosa La Barbera; Color: Dario Calabria

The End

Skipping Trick

WOW, THIS IS FUN!

AND YOU ARE REALLY GOOD AT JUMPING!

SWISH

SWISH

!

ELSA, CAN I TRY TOO?

OF COURSE! YOU JUST HAVE TO JUMP AND LET THE ROPE TURN!

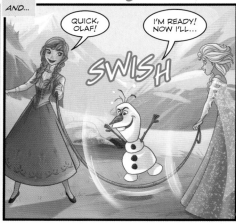

AND...

QUICK, OLAF!

I'M READY! NOW I'LL...

SWISH

JUUUMP...OOOPS!

SWOOSH

?!?

DID I DO IT RIGHT? I DON'T THINK I JUMPED IN TIME!

?!?

Manuscript: Tea Orsi; Layout: Zanon Alberto; Cleanup: Letizia Algeri; Color: Dario Calabria

The End

EVERYTHING IN ITS PLACE

ANNA AND KRISTOFF OFFERED TO HELP OAKEN DELIVER SOME ITEMS TO THE ICE HARVESTERS...

I'M EXCITED TO SEE MY BUDDIES!

AS SOON AS WE ARE DONE LOADING THE SLEIGH WE CAN GET GOING!

THAT COULD TAKE A WHILE...

COME ON! IT WILL BE AS EASY AS PACKING A SUITCASE.

Manuscript: Tea Orsi; Layout: Alberto Zanon; Cleanup: Veronica Di Lorenzo; Color: MichelAngela World

THE KEY IS TO FIND THE **RIGHT** PLACE FOR EACH OBJECT...

THE HEAVIEST MUST BE LOADED FIRST...

PANT!

... AND THE MOST FRAGILE CAREFULLY PLACED ON TOP, SO THEY DON'T GET CRUSHED!

YAH, THAT MAKES SENSE!

AFTER SOME METICULOUS WORK...

I THINK WE'RE READY TO GO!

WAIT! I MUST GET ONE MORE ITEM...

HOO-HOO! HERE IS AN ICE-SHAPING MACHINE OF MY OWN MAKING! I KEPT IT SAFE, OUTSIDE THE BACK OF THE STORE.

I PROMISED THE ICE-HARVESTERS...

GASP!

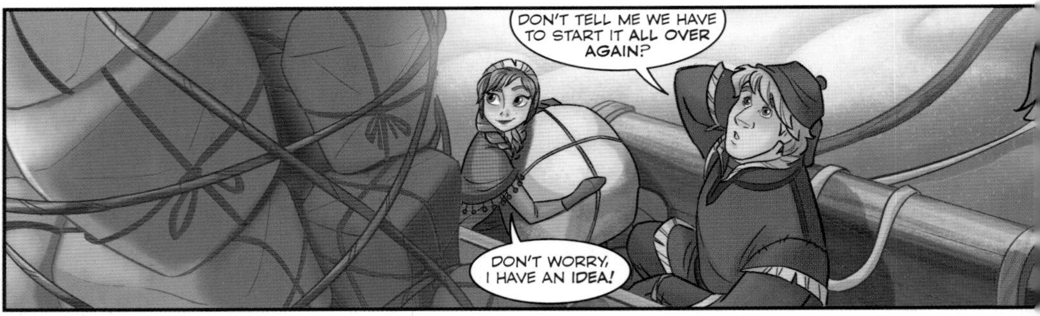
DON'T TELL ME WE HAVE TO START IT ALL OVER AGAIN?
DON'T WORRY, I HAVE AN IDEA!

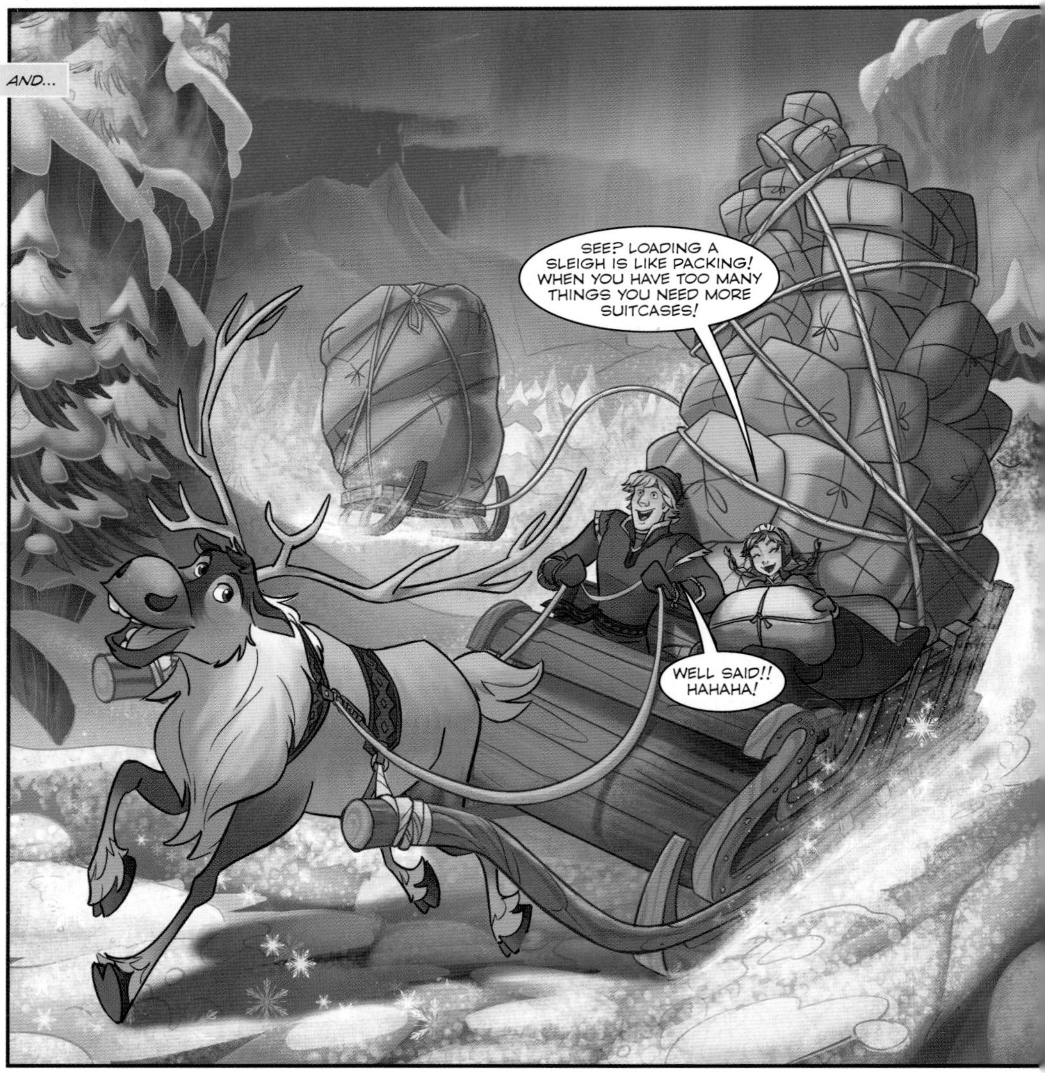
AND...
SEE? LOADING A SLEIGH IS LIKE PACKING! WHEN YOU HAVE TOO MANY THINGS YOU NEED MORE SUITCASES!
WELL SAID!! HAHAHA!

The End

THE BEAST ON THE BLUFF

THIS IS IT!

THIS IS THE SAME SPOT WHERE SVEN AND I WOULD CAMP WITH THE ICE HARVESTERS WHEN WE WERE KIDS.

LET'S PUT UP THE TENT!

FIRST THINGS FIRST, OLAF. WE'RE GONNA LOSE DAYLIGHT SOON--WE'D BETTER BUILD A FIRE SO WE'RE NOT FUMBLING AROUND IN THE DARK.

OOH, I CAN DO THAT!

WHY DON'T YOU HELP ME COLLECT FIREWOOD INSTEAD?

LATER...

OWOOOOO

THIS IS MORE LIKE IT.

TIME TO ROAST THE CHESTNUTS!

WAIT--DO YOU HEAR THAT HOWLING?

MAYBE IT WAS JUST THE WIND... BUT IT REMINDS ME OF SOMETHING THE ICE HARVESTERS USED TO DO BY THE CAMPFIRE--

--TELL SPOOKY CAMPFIRE STORIES!

I LOVE SPOOKY CAMPFIRE STORIES! WHAT IS A SPOOKY CAMPFIRE STORY?

anuscript: Joe Caramagna; Layout: Ciro Cangialosi; Pencil: Manuela Razzi and Michela Frare; Ink/Paint: Michelangela_World

MANY YEARS AGO, ON A NIGHT JUST LIKE THIS, ICE HARVESTERS WERE CAMPING ON THIS *VERY* SPOT WHEN THEY HEARD A *HOWL* IN THE DISTANCE.

AT FIRST, THEY BLAMED THE WIND, BUT SOME OF THEM CLAIMED TO HAVE SEEN A BIG...FURRY...SCARY *SNOW BEAST!*

OOH, THAT'S A GOOD STORY! CAN I GO NEXT?

MY STORY WASN'T FINISHED YET, BUT... SURE, WHY NOT?

ONE NIGHT, A SNOWMAN AND A REINDEER AND A HUMAN WENT CAMPING. AND THEY SET UP A TENT--BUT *FIRST* THEY STARTED A FIRE-- BUT FIRST THEY HAD TO COLLECT FIREWOOD...

SOUNDS FAMILIAR.

SUDDENLY, A *SCARY* BEAST CAME! AND IT WAS *BIG*, AND *SCARY*, AND *FURRY*, AND...AND *SCARY*...

THIS SOUNDS A LOT LIKE MY STORY...

...AND THE BEAST TOOK THEIR *FOOD* AND RAN OFF INTO THE WOODS WITH IT!

WAIT A MINUTE...*THAT* PART'S NEW...

OUR *FOOD!* IT'S *GONE!*

OLAF, DID YOU SEE WHAT HAPPENED TO OUR STUFF?

I TOLD YOU--IT WAS A *SCARY BEAST.*

BUT THAT'S *IMPOSSIBLE,* I MADE THAT STORY UP. THERE IS NO SUCH BEAST!

BUT THERE *WAS* ONE. IT CREPT UP TO THE SLEIGH, SNIFFED THE BAG OF FOOD, THEN DRAGGED IT AWAY!

WHAT DID IT *LOOK* LIKE?

I TOLD YOU, IT WAS BIG AND SCARY AND FURRY AND SCARY--

IT TOOK *EVERYTHING.*

ACTUALLY, IT DID LEAVE *SOMETHING* BEHIND-- *TRACKS!*

LET'S GO!

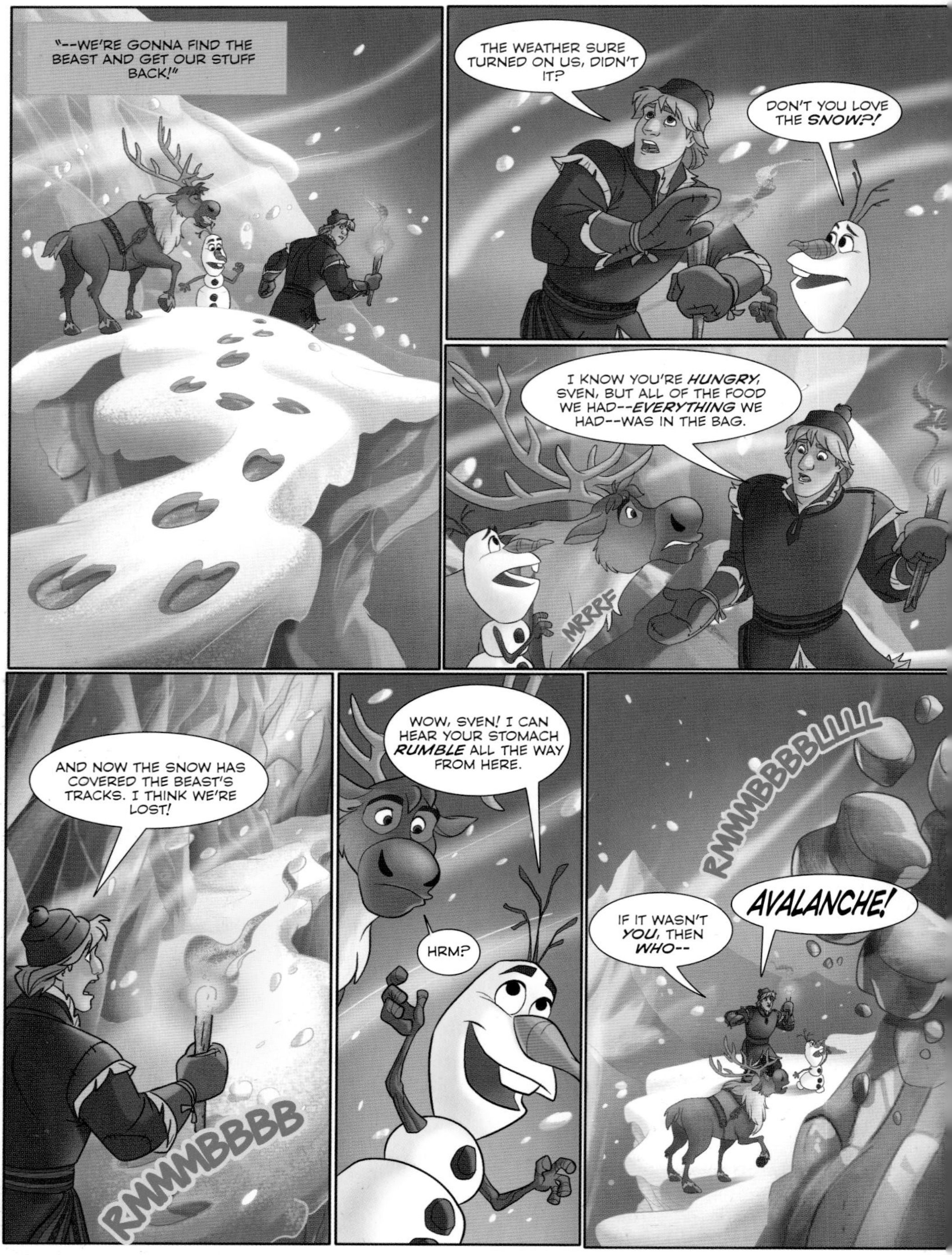
"--WE'RE GONNA FIND THE BEAST AND GET OUR STUFF BACK!"
THE WEATHER SURE TURNED ON US, DIDN'T IT?
DON'T YOU LOVE THE SNOW?!
I KNOW YOU'RE HUNGRY, SVEN, BUT ALL OF THE FOOD WE HAD--EVERYTHING WE HAD--WAS IN THE BAG.
MRRRF
AND NOW THE SNOW HAS COVERED THE BEAST'S TRACKS. I THINK WE'RE LOST!
RMMMBBBB
WOW, SVEN! I CAN HEAR YOUR STOMACH RUMBLE ALL THE WAY FROM HERE.
HRM?
RMMMBBBBLLLL
IF IT WASN'T YOU, THEN WHO--
AVALANCHE!

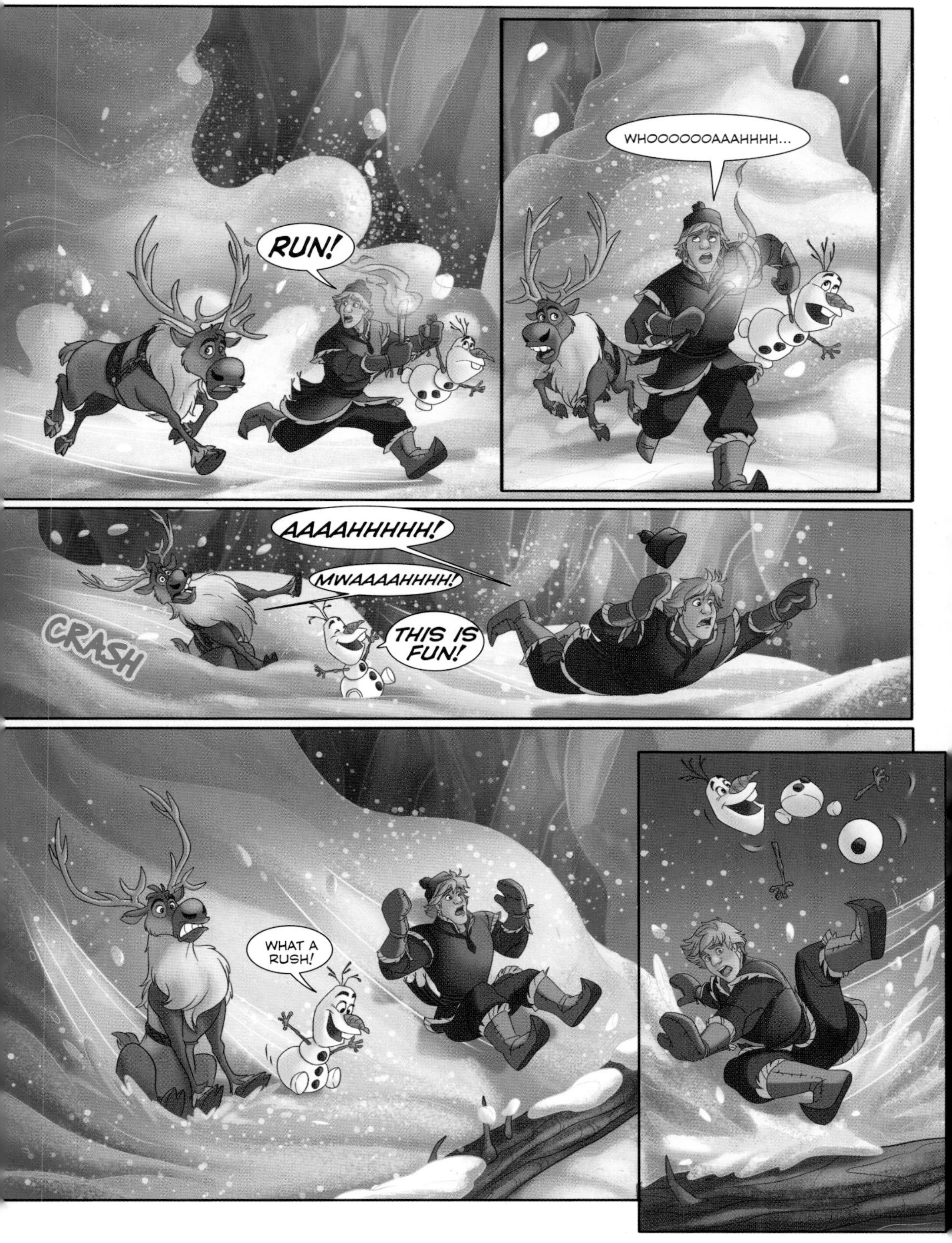
RUN!
WHOOOOOOAAAHHHH...
AAAAHHHHH!
MWAAAAHHHH!
CRASH
THIS IS FUN!
WHAT A RUSH!

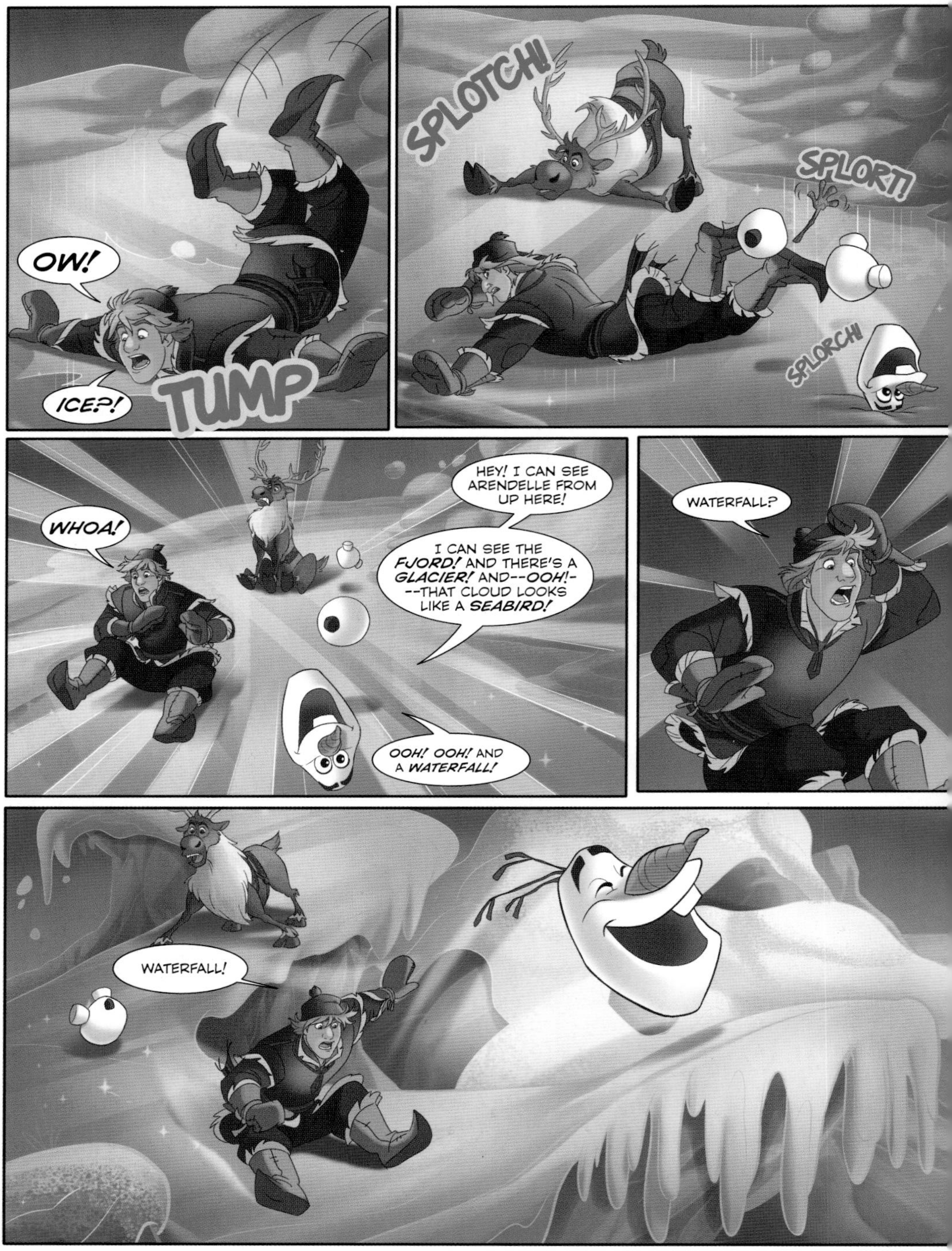
OW!
ICE?!
TUMP
SPLOTCH!
SPLORT!
SPLORCH!
WHOA!
HEY! I CAN SEE ARENDELLE FROM UP HERE!
I CAN SEE THE FJORD! AND THERE'S A GLACIER! AND--OOH!- --THAT CLOUD LOOKS LIKE A SEABIRD!
OOH! OOH! AND A WATERFALL!
WATERFALL?
WATERFALL!

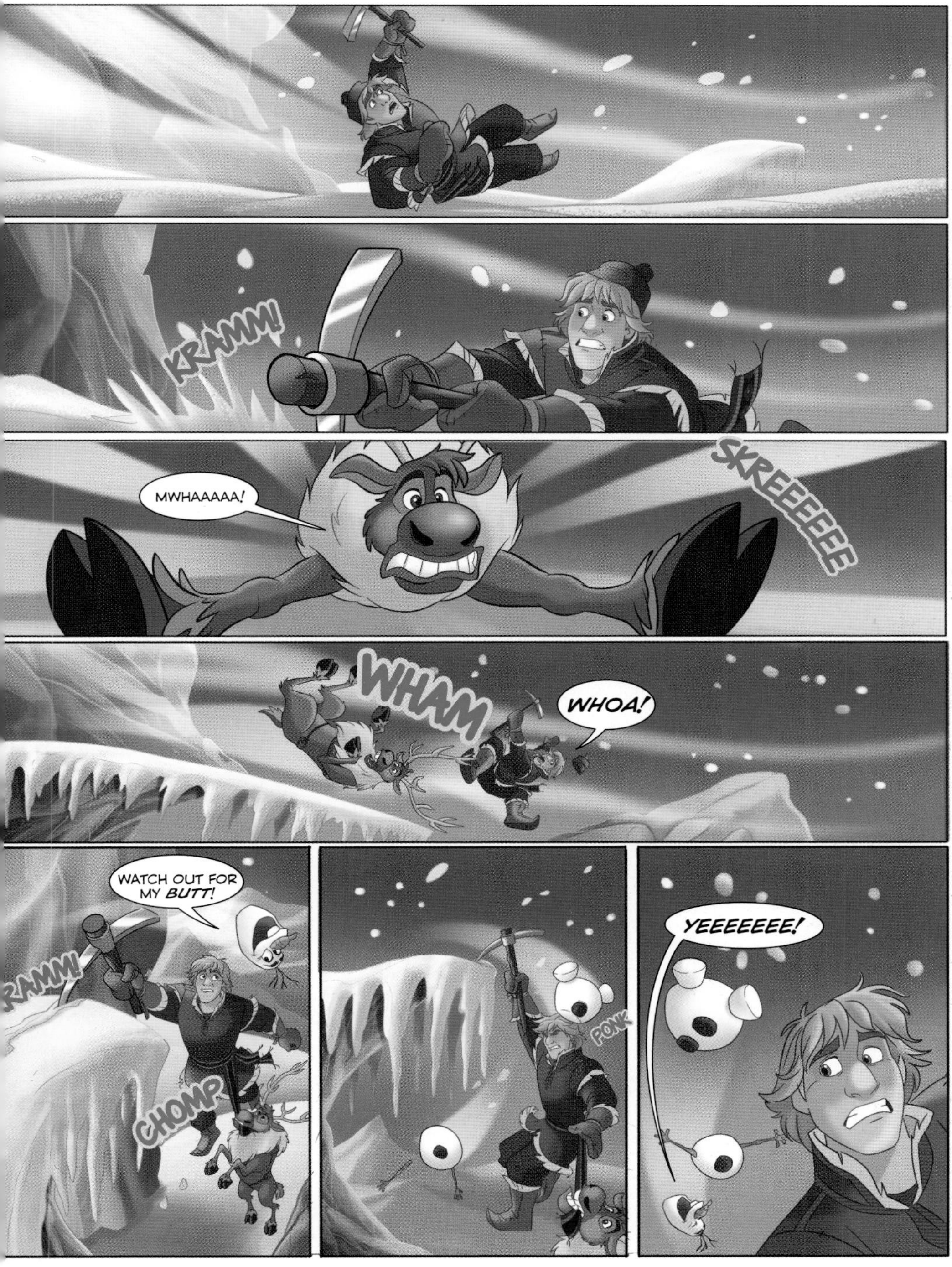
KRAMM!
MWHAAAAA!
SKREEEEEEE
WHAM
WHOA!
WATCH OUT FOR MY *BUTT*!
RAMM!
CHOMP
PONK
YEEEEEEE!

...OLAF?

I'M *OKAY!*

ACTUALLY, THE SNOW DOWN HERE IS DEEP AND SOFT. IT WAS LIKE LANDING ON A BIG *PILLOW!*

OKAY, SVEN, I'M GONNA COUNT TO *THREE* AND--

--PLEASE DON'T LOOK AT ME LIKE THAT. I DON'T LIKE THIS PLAN EITHER, BUT WE CAN'T STAY HERE...

OLAF MADE IT, AND HE CAN'T FEEL PAIN, BUT...

...THREEEEEEEEEEE!

...WE CAN'T GO BACK *UP.*

SO, READY? ONE...*TWO*...

KRRRRKKK

HEY, *LOOK!* IT'S THE BEAST'S TRACKS!

COME ON!

THAT WAS *FUN!* CAN WE DO IT AGAIN?

SHUFFT

SHUFFT

THEY END HERE-- IN THIS *CAVE.*

I'M NOT LEAVING WITHOUT OUR FOOD...

...IF WE CAN *FIND* IT. I CAN'T SEE A *THING* IN THERE.

I NEED TO IMPROVISE...

SKRITCH
SKRITCH

HELLO? ANYONE *HOME?* I THINK YOU HAVE SOMETHING THAT BELONGS TO US.

YOU SEE, MY FRIENDS AND I WERE CAMPING, AND WHEN YOU CAME BY EARLIER, YOU MAY HAVE TAKEN OUR *FOOD*. BY MISTAKE, I'M SURE. AND, WELL, WE SORT OF *NEED* IT.

HELLO? IS ANYBODY--

AAAAAAHHHHH!

OH, HELLO! WHAT'S YOUR NAME?

GAHHH!

KRISTOFF!

CHOMP

AHHH! THE BEAST GOT ME! THE BEAST--

--GOT ME! IT SAVED ME!

SO YOU'RE THE "BEAST" WHO STOLE OUR FOOD, EH?

EASY, SVEN--THIS MOOSE IS OUT HERE ALL ON HIS OWN AND WAS PROBABLY HUNGRY...

...ISN'T THAT RIGHT, FRIEND?

LET'S EAT, NOW!

THAT'S A GREAT IDEA, OLAF. IN FACT...

"...I THINK WE SHOULD ALL ENJOY OUR MEAL TOGETHER."

...IT TURNS OUT THAT THE SNOW BEAST WAS IN REALITY A BEAR, HOWLING BECAUSE IT HAD A *CAVITY* IN ITS FANGS AND WAS IN A LOT OF *PAIN*...

...SO THE HARVESTERS USED THEIR PICKAXES TO REMOVE THE ROTTEN TOOTH, AND THEY ALL LIVED HAPPILY--

--YES, OLAF?

OH! OH! I KNOW A GOOD STORY! ME NEXT!

ONE NIGHT, A SNOWMAN AND A REINDEER AND A HUMAN WENT CAMPING--

I THINK I'VE HEARD THIS BEFORE...

--WHEN SUDDENLY, A SCARY BEAST TOOK THEIR FOOD AND RAN OFF INTO THE WOODS WITH IT!

THEY FOLLOWED ITS TRACKS TO FIND THAT IT WAS ONLY A MOOSE--

--WHO JUST NEEDED SOME FOOD AND WARM HUGS.

THEY ALL BECAME FRIENDS AND LIVED *HAPPILY EVER AFTER!*

YOU KNOW WHAT, OLAF?

THAT'S THE BEST CAMPFIRE STORY I'VE EVER HEARD.

The End

150

ALMOST READY

THIS MORNING, SOME IMPORTANT GUESTS ARE COMING TO THE CASTLE...

ANNA! IT'S LATE!

BUT INSIDE THE ROOM...

GASP! I'M COMING!

THUD TUMP BANG

JUST A... AHHH... SECOND!

ARE YOU OKAY?

YES, AND... I'M READY!

ERM...

YIKES! I GUESS I'M NOT AS READY AS I THOUGHT.

DON'T WORRY! I'M HERE TO HELP YOU...

Manuscript: Tea Orsi; Layout: Marino Gentile; Cleanup:Nicoletta Baldari; Paint: Dario Calabria

The End

CAMPING NIGHT

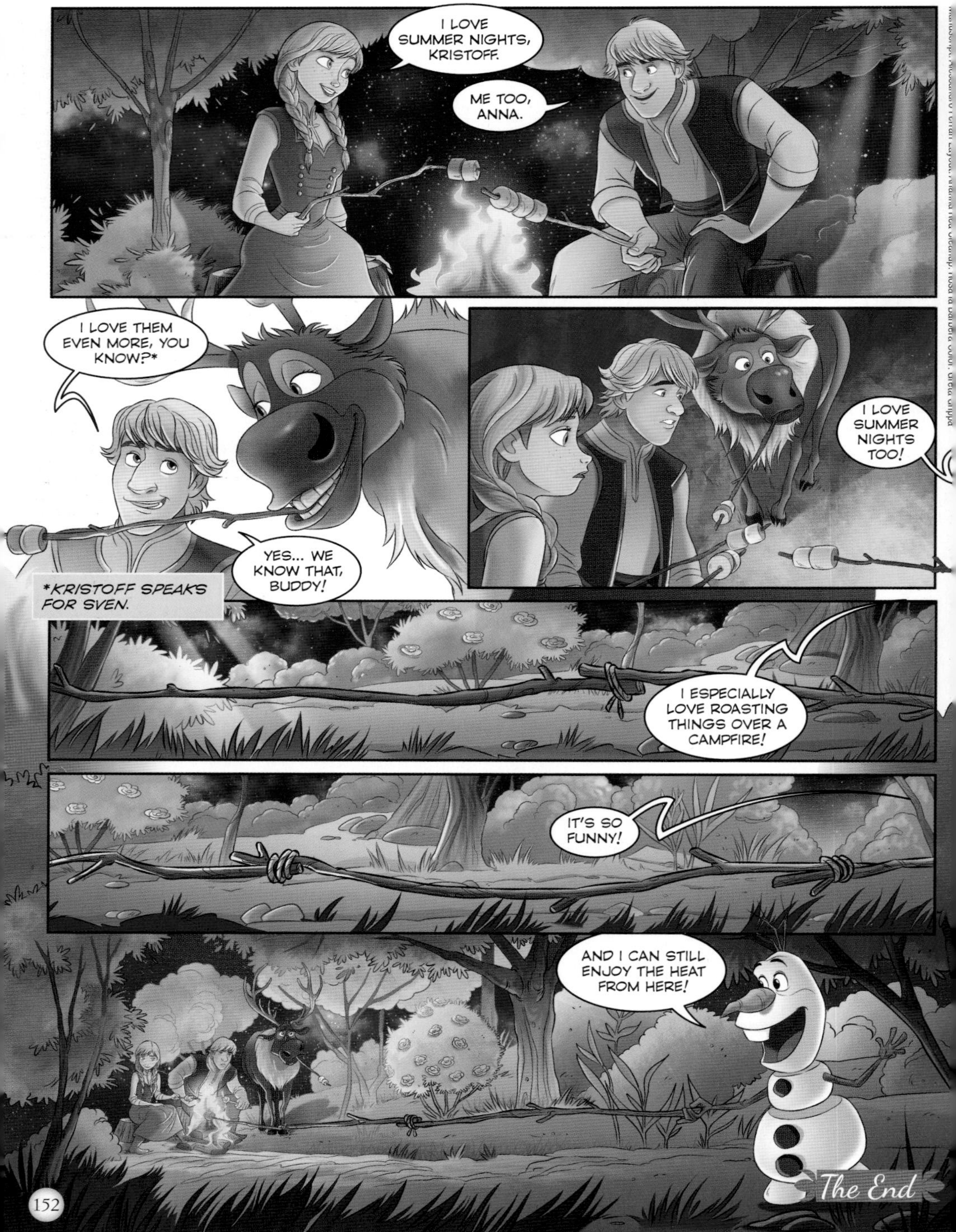
I LOVE SUMMER NIGHTS, KRISTOFF.
ME TOO, ANNA.
I LOVE THEM EVEN MORE, YOU KNOW?*
YES... WE KNOW THAT, BUDDY!
*KRISTOFF SPEAKS FOR SVEN.
I LOVE SUMMER NIGHTS TOO!
I ESPECIALLY LOVE ROASTING THINGS OVER A CAMPFIRE!
IT'S SO FUNNY!
AND I CAN STILL ENJOY THE HEAT FROM HERE!
The End

An Artful Solution

ANNA HAS JUST WOKEN UP, WHEN...

BRRR! IT'S SO COLD...

HUH?! LEAVING THE DOOR OPEN IS NOT A GOOD IDEA WITH THIS WEATHER!

OH, THE LOCK SEEMS STUCK...

WHAT IS A LOCK?

IT'S THE THING THAT KEEPS THE DOOR CLOSED, OLAF!

ANNA CALLS ELSA, AND...

BANG

IT DOESN'T MOVE!

MAYBE YOU ARE MAKING TOO MUCH NOISE AND THE LOCK IS SCARED!

Manuscript: Tea Orsi; Layout: Emilio Urbano; Clean up: Marino Gentile; Ink: Michela Frare; Color: Ekaterina Maximenko

WE CAN TEMPORARILY TIE THE HANDLES TOGETHER!

YOU'RE RIGHT! I'LL GET SOME STRINGS!

BUT...

WE HAVE NO STRING LEFT! BUT I'VE FOUND THESE!

HUH?!

OH, YOU MUST FEEL REALLY COLD!

NO! WE'LL USE THE SCARVES TO TIE THE HANDLES TOGETHER!

GOOD IDEA, ANNA!

AND, AFTER SOME HARD WORK...

GREAT! THOSE KNOTS ARE REALLY TIGHT!

OH, YES! NOW OPENING THE DOOR IS ALMOST IMPOSSIBLE!

IT LOOKS BEAUTIFUL!

BUT, JUST THEN...

KNOCK

WE ARE HERE! CAN YOU OPEN THE DOOR, PLEASE?

WHY IS IT TAKING SO LONG?

OOPS!

The End

154

LET'S GET CREATIVE!

ELSA AND ANNA ARE VISITING OAKEN...

HOO HOO! DO YOU LIKE MY NEW INVENTION?

IT'S REALLY UNUSUAL!

BUT...WHAT IS IT?

IT'S A TEATIME MACHINE!

IT CAN OFFER EVERYTHING YOU NEED FOR TEA!

MMM... HOT COCOA!

... AND COOKIES!

THIS INVENTION IS AMAZING!

THEN IT'S ALL YOURS! I'LL TAKE IT TO THE CASTLE FOR YOU!

Manuscript: Tea Orsi; Layout: Emilio Urbano; Cleanup: Manuela Razzi and Letizia Algeri; Color: Maria Claudia Di Genova

I'D REALLY LIKE TO BE ABLE TO BUILD SUCH USEFUL **CONTRAPTIONS** LIKE YOU, OAKEN!

WHY DON'T YOU TRY?

YES, WE'LL BUILD SOME **CONTRAPTIONS** AND THEN WE WILL SHOW THEM TO YOU!

MMM... THEN I HAVE AN IDEA...

...WE'LL ORGANIZE A **CREATIVITY EXHIBITION** AT THE CASTLE NEXT WEEK!

YES! AND OAKEN WILL CHOOSE **THE BEST INVENTION!**

LATER...

WOW!

EVERYONE CAN BUILD THEIR OWN USEFUL **CONTRAPTIONS.** AND NEXT WEEK...

WE'LL HAVE AN EXHIBITION AT THE CASTLE AND OAKEN WILL CHOOSE THE BEST INVENTION!

I HAVE A GREAT IDEA ALREADY!

SOON, EVERYONE IS WORKING...

CAN WE BUILD AN INVENTION THAT MAKES SUMMER?

MMM... THAT MIGHT BE TRICKY!

BUT WE CAN MAKE A CRYSTAL MOBILE TO CATCH THE SUNLIGHT!

OHHHH! I LOVE THE COLORS OF SUNLIGHT!

AND, ON THE DAY OF THE EXHIBITION...

IT'S NEARLY DONE!

WHAT KIND OF INVENTION IS THIS?

IT'S A MAKE-WAY-FOR-THE-SLEIGH!

OH YEAH! EVERYONE WILL HEAR US WHEN WE'RE APPROACHING!

CLANG CLANG

WE'LL TEST IT LATER! WE'RE HELPING OAKEN CARRY HIS CONTRAPTION TO THE CASTLE!

IN FACT...

SWOOSH

SDENG
CLANG

SHR

SOUNDS LIKE YOUR SLEIGH NEEDS FIXING!

NO, IT'S JUST ANNA'S INVENTION!

BUT...

BONK

CRASH

OH NO!

WHOA, SVEN!

MY MACHINE IS DESTROYED!

WE'RE NOT FAR FROM THE CASTLE!

WE'LL TAKE IT THERE AND FIX IT!

OH DEAR! WHAT HAPPENED?

WE NEED YOUR HELP TO FIX OAKEN'S MACHINE!

I'LL SAVE THE HOT-COCOA TAP!

SCREECH

THE CUPS STILL WORK!

CRUNCH

BANG BANG

THANK YOU!

AFTER SOME MORE WORK, EVERYONE IS READY...

HOO HOO! WELCOME TO THE CREATIVITY EXHIBITION. YOUR CONTRAPTIONS ARE SO INVENTIVE!

IT WILL BE DIFFICULT TO CHOOSE THE BEST ONE!

IF YOU DON'T MIND, I CAN GIVE YOU A LITTLE HELP...

THE BEST INVENTION IS ...THE **TEATIME MACHINE**, BECAUSE EVERYONE WORKED TOGETHER TO REPAIR IT!

CONGRATULATIONS, OAKEN!

HURRAY FOR TEAMWORK!

THANK YOU! YOU MADE MY INVENTION EVEN BETTER!

AND NOW...LET'S CELEBRATE!

HURRAY FOR OAKEN!

HURRAY!

CLAP

CLAP

The End

BIRTHDAY MEMORIES

TODAY IS ANNA'S *BIRTHDAY!*

WHAT A PERFECT DAY! I CAN'T WAIT TO CELEBRATE WITH MY FRIENDS!

BUT...

WHOOSH

BRRR! WHERE IS THIS COLD AIR COMING FROM? WHAT'S GOING ON?

HAPPY BIRTHDAY, ANNA!

ELSA?! I KNEW YOU HAD SOMETHING TO DO WITH THIS SUMMER COLD!

SO... TELL ME ABOUT YOUR PLAN!

YOU'LL FIND OUT SOON, BUT I'LL GIVE YOU A CLUE...

ginal Story by: Erica David; Adaptation: Tea Orsi; Layout: Emilio Urbano; Clean: Elisabetta Melaranci; Color: MichelAngela World

ON THE MORNING OF YOUR FIFTH BIRTHDAY...

"YOU WOKE UP TO A SOFT SPRINKLE OF **SNOWFLAKES** ABOVE YOUR BED. THEY WERE DRIFTING DOWN FROM THE CEILING, BUT..."

OHHHHH!

"... THEY WEREN'T JUST ANY SNOWFLAKES. EACH ONE WAS A TINY SCULPTURE!"

THAT ONE LOOKS LIKE ELSA! AND THOSE ARE SNOWMAN SNOWFLAKES!

"THEN YOU FOLLOWED THE **SNOWFLAKE PATH** THROUGH THE CASTLE, AND..."

HAPPY BIRTHDAY, ANNA!

"IT WAS TIME TO BUILD A *SPECIAL SNOWMAN* FOR YOUR BIRTHDAY!"

"WE ROLLED THE SNOW INTO GIANT SNOWBALLS..."

"... AND STACKED THEM ON TOP OF EACH OTHER."

"THEN YOU WANTED TO STICK ON THE BUTTON EYES AND CARROT NOSE..."

"... BUT YOU NEEDED A LITTLE HELP."

"IT WAS SO MUCH FUN!"

OH, I'D LOVE TO MAKE A SNOWMAN, EVEN IF IT IS SUMMER!

I KNOW! SO... THIS YEAR MY GIFT MIGHT NOT BE VERY ORIGINAL, BUT...

... I'M SURE THAT TOGETHER WE WILL ALL ENJOY IT EVEN MORE!

HAPPY BIRTHDAY, ANNA!

THIS IS GOING TO BE AN AMAZING DAY!

The End

THE WAKE UP CLOCK

Manuscript: Tea Orsi; Layout: Caterina Giorgetti; Clean: Sara Storino; Color: Silvano Scolari

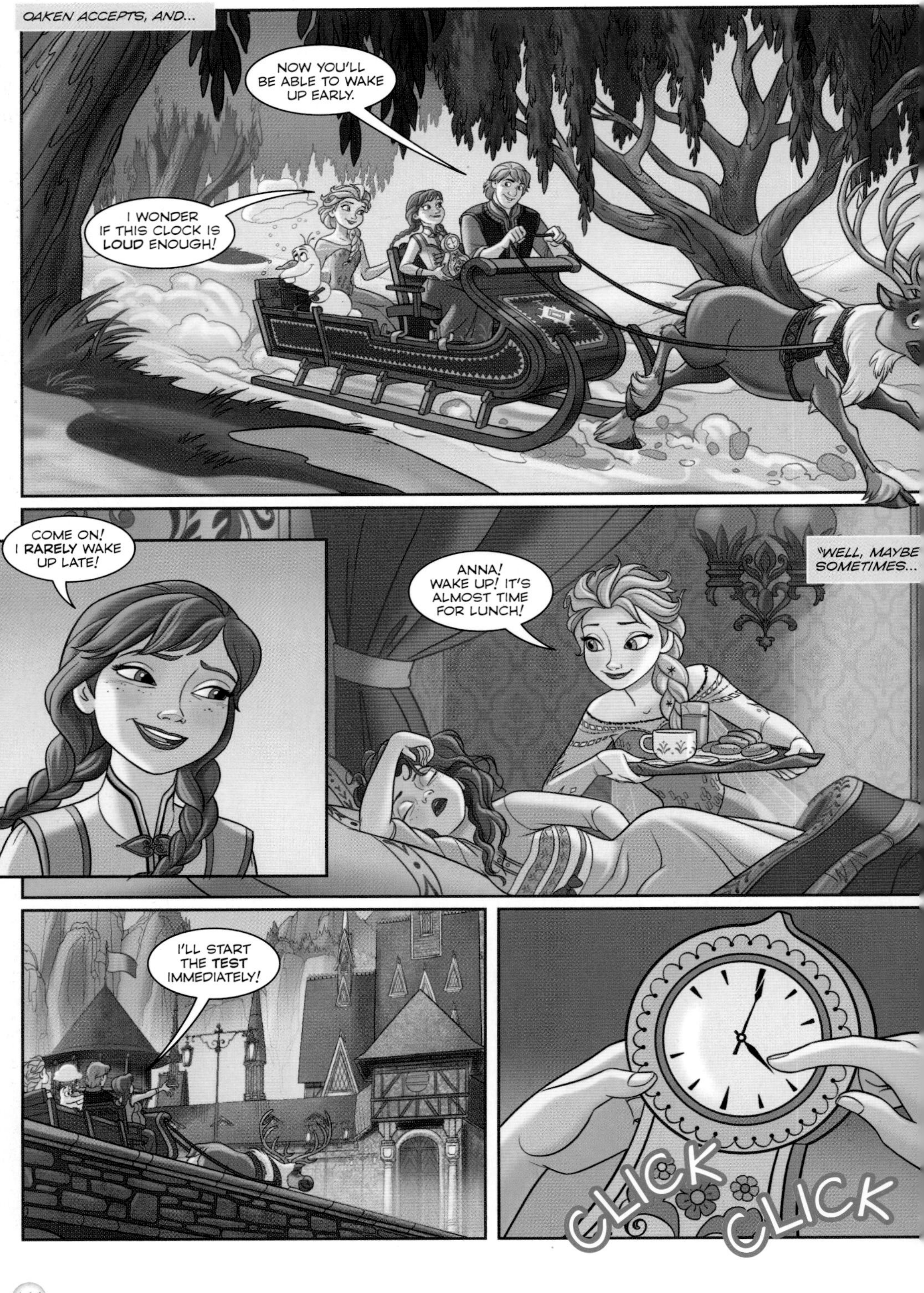
OAKEN ACCEPTS, AND...
NOW YOU'LL BE ABLE TO WAKE UP EARLY.
I WONDER IF THIS CLOCK IS **LOUD** ENOUGH!
COME ON! I **RARELY** WAKE UP LATE!
"WELL, MAYBE SOMETIMES...
ANNA! WAKE UP! IT'S ALMOST TIME FOR LUNCH!
I'LL START THE **TEST** IMMEDIATELY!
CLICK
CLICK

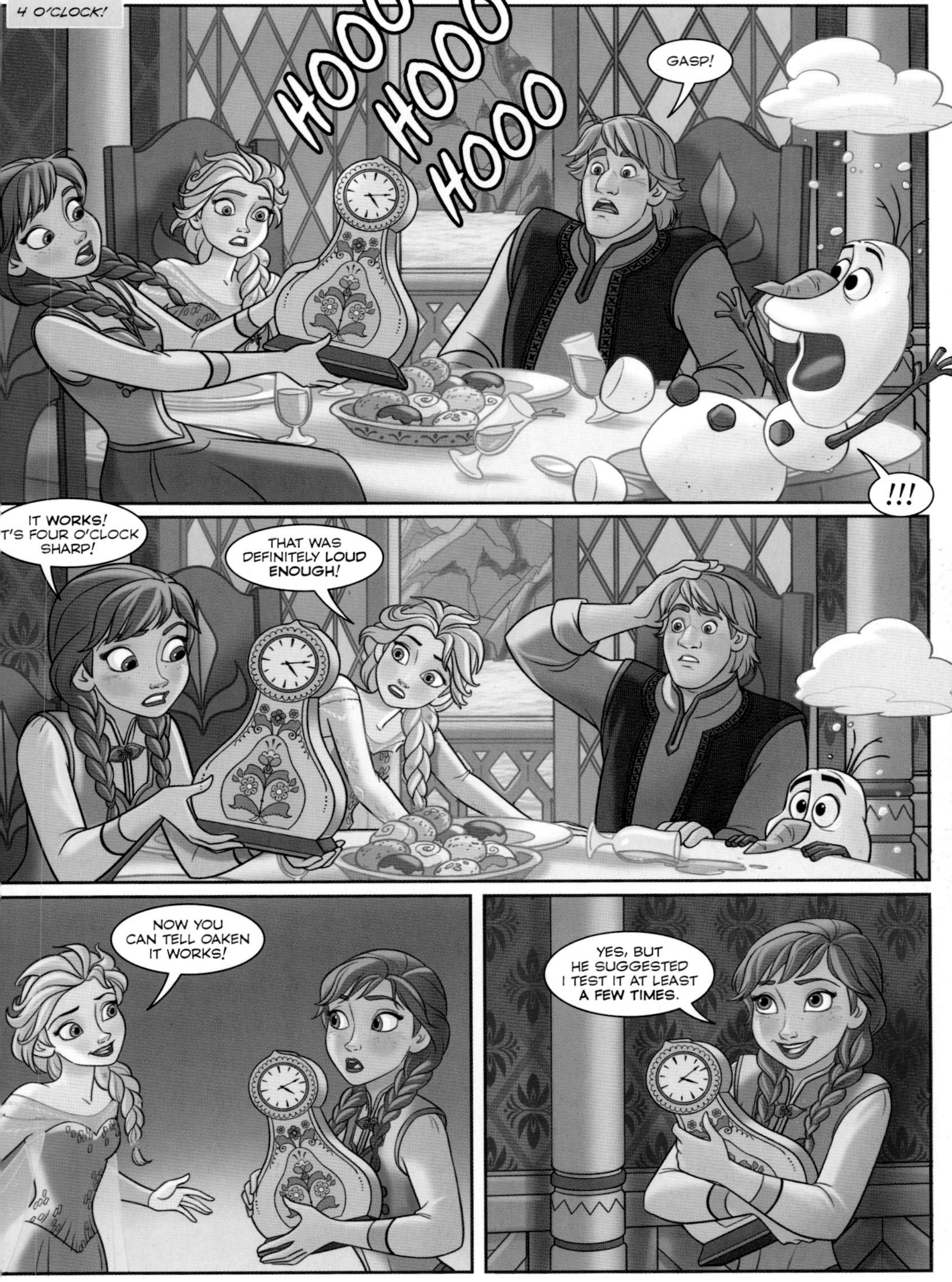
4 O'CLOCK!
HOOO HOOO HOOO
GASP!
!!!
IT WORKS! T'S FOUR O'CLOCK SHARP!
THAT WAS DEFINITELY LOUD ENOUGH!
NOW YOU CAN TELL OAKEN IT WORKS!
YES, BUT HE SUGGESTED I TEST IT AT LEAST A FEW TIMES.

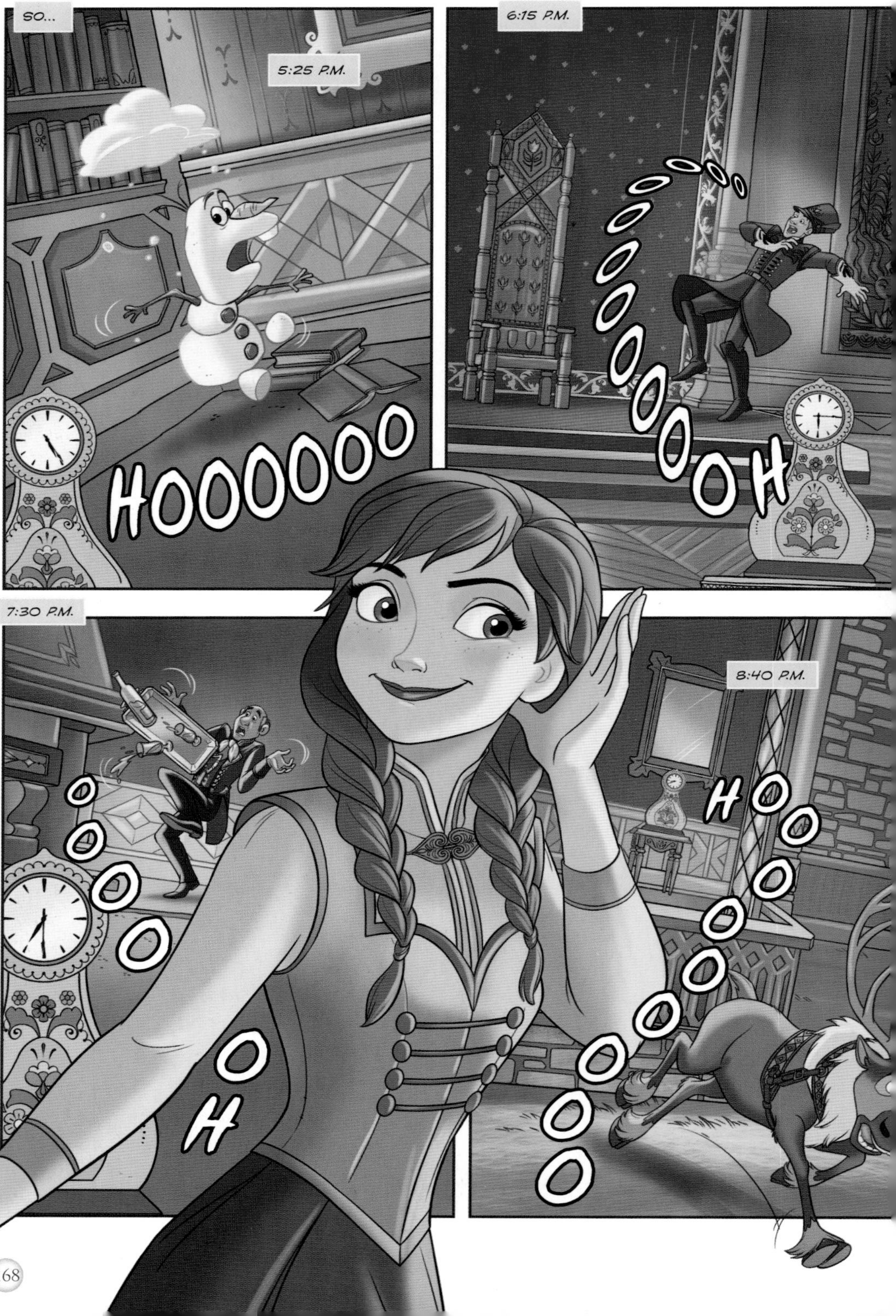
SO...
5:25 P.M.
HOOOOOOO
6:15 P.M.
OOOOOOOOOOOOOH
7:30 P.M.
OOOOOOH
8:40 P.M.
HOOOOOOOOOO

LATER, AFTER MANY UCCESSFUL ATTEMPTS...

GREAT! I CAN'T WAIT TO TELL OAKEN THAT HIS CLOCK WORKS PERFECTLY!

THEN, YOU CAN USE IT TO WAKE UP EARLY TOMORROW.

NT...

THIS IS FUN!

OLAF, SVEN! BE CAREFUL!

FWOOOOSH

BONK!

GASP!

HOOOOOO

THUD

I HOPE IT'S NOT BROKEN!

BUT WE SHOULD STOP THIS NOISE!

SOUNDS TO ME IT'S WORKING TOO WELL!

HOOOOOOOO

HOW CAN WE STOP IT?

HOOOOOO

I HAVE AN IDEA.

THE CLOCK BELONGS TO OAKEN, WE CAN'T BREAK IT!

HOOO OOO O

YOU'RE RIGHT, BUT THIS NOISE WILL WAKE UP ALL ARENDELLE!

OOOOOO

I THINK WE SHOULD JUST WAIT FOR THE GEARS TO STOP TURNING!

HOOOOO

THE SOUND WILL BE SOFTER IF WE COVER THE CLOCK!

HOOOOOOO

OH, YOU ARE PUTTING IT TO BED.

UT...

HOOOOOOOO

ERM... DID YOU SAY SOFTER?

I GUESS WE SHOULD FIND ANOTHER SOLUTION...

HOOOOOO

LET'S PUT IT INSIDE THERE!

I'M NOT SO SURE...

HOOOO

BUT...

HOOOOO

YIKES!

HMMM, STILL NOISY!

OUR FRIENDS KEEP TRYING, BUT...

HOOOOOOOOO

I'M AFRAID THIS SOUND WILL NEVER END!

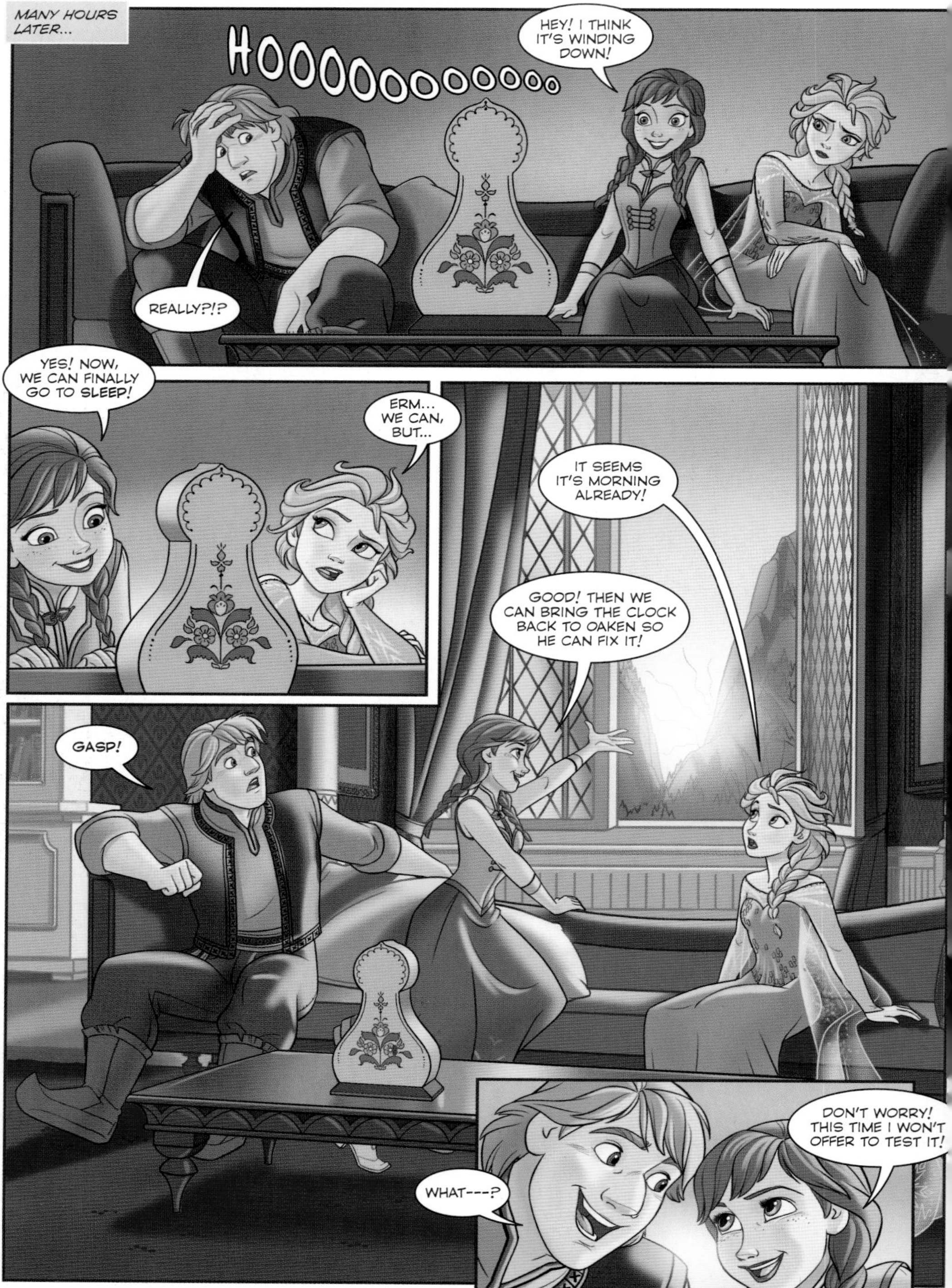
MANY HOURS LATER...
HOOOOOOOOOOoo
HEY! I THINK IT'S WINDING DOWN!
REALLY?!?
YES! NOW, WE CAN FINALLY GO TO SLEEP!
ERM... WE CAN, BUT...
IT SEEMS IT'S MORNING ALREADY!
GOOD! THEN WE CAN BRING THE CLOCK BACK TO OAKEN SO HE CAN FIX IT!
GASP!
WHAT---?
DON'T WORRY! THIS TIME I WON'T OFFER TO TEST IT!

The End

THE SKATED MESSAGE

anuscript: Tea Orsi; Layout and cleanup: Nicoletta Baldari;
:olor: Dario Calabria

The End

A Cool Surprise

AT THE ICE PALACE, OLAF HAS A SURPRISE IN STORE FOR MARSHMALLOW!

JUST A FEW MORE STEPS...

HERE WE ARE! NOW YOU CAN TAKE OF THE BLINDFOLD.

TA-DA!

UH?!

SNIFF! SNIFF!

ATCHOO!!!

AWWW! I DIDN'T KNOW YOU WERE ALLERGIC TO FLOWERS! THAT'S QUITE A SNEEZE!

Manuscript: Valentina Cambi; Layout: Alberto Zanon; Cleanup: Letizia Algeri; Color: MichelAngela World

The End

OLAF'S PASTIME

IT'S A QUIET MORNING AT THE CASTLE...

THANK YOU, OLAF!

YOUR MUSIC IS SO NICE, KRISTOFF!

PLINN PLINN

PLAYING MY LUTE IS MY FAVORITE PASTIME!

I LOVE PASTIMES! WHAT IS A PASTIME?

IT'S AN ACTIVITY YOU DO IN YOUR FREE TIME!

SOMETHING THAT MAKES YOU FEEL HAPPY!

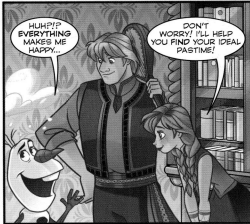

HUH?!? EVERYTHING MAKES ME HAPPY...

DON'T WORRY! I'LL HELP YOU FIND YOUR IDEAL PASTIME!

anuscript: Tea Orsi; Layout: Alberto Zanon ; Cleanup: Nicoletta Baldari; Color: Manuela Nerolini, Ekaterina Maximenko and Ekaterina Myshalova

MINUTES LATER...

I'LL SHOW YOU SOME OF MY PASTIMES. MAYBE YOU'LL LIKE THEM TOO!

THAT SOUNDS LIKE FUN!

I LOVE TO CLIMB TREES!

DO YOU WANT TO TRY?

SURE! BUT I'LL CLIMB IN A DIFFERENT WAY!

LOOK!

I'VE CLIMBED THE TREE!

ERM...YEAH! MAYBE WE CAN TRY SOMETHING ELSE...

SO, WHAT ARE YOU PAINTING?

ANOTHER OLAF!

IT EVEN HAS **REAL SNOW** ON IT!

HUH?!? WOW!

LET'S GO!

SO YOU THINK **PAINTING** MAY BE YOUR FAVORITE PASTIME?

I LOVE IT! BUT I'D LIKE TO **TRY** SOMETHING ELSE TOO!

HMMM... OKAY ...

SWOOSH

AND...

I LOVE TO MAKE SNOW SCULPTURES!

ARE YOU ENJOYING IT TOO, OLAF?

YES! IT'S GREAT!

BUT MAYBE WE SHOULD TRY SOMETHING MORE

YOU CAN ASK KRISTOFF TO SHOW YOU HIS PASTIMES TOO!

YES, AFTER ALL IT ALL STARTED FROM HIM!

IN THE GARDEN...

BESIDE PLAYING MY LUTE, I LIKE RIDING SVEN!

AND SVEN'S PASTIME IS KISSING MY CARROT NOSE!

AND I LOVE HIKING!

LET'S DO IT TOGETHER!

LATER, ON THE MOUNTAINS...

SO, YOU THINK THIS COULD BE YOUR FAVORITE PASTIME, OLAF?

YES, IT COULD BE!

JUST LIKE THE OTHER THINGS WE'VE DONE TODAY!

REALLY?

YOU HELPED ME FIND THE BEST PASTIME EVER!

WHAT'S YOUR FAVORITE THING WE'VE DONE TODAY?

EVERYTHING!

179

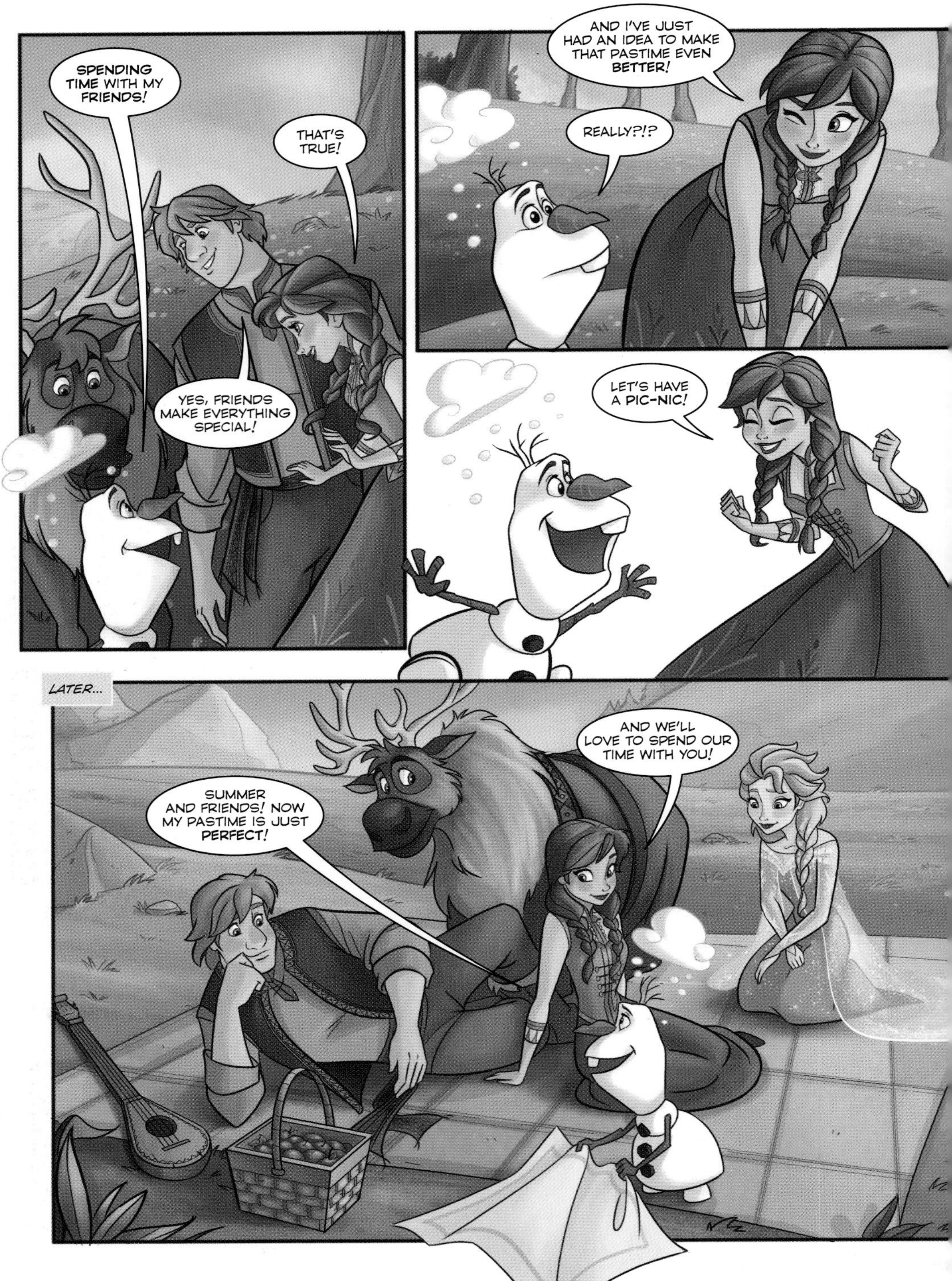
SPENDING TIME WITH MY FRIENDS!
THAT'S TRUE!
YES, FRIENDS MAKE EVERYTHING SPECIAL!
AND I'VE JUST HAD AN IDEA TO MAKE THAT PASTIME EVEN BETTER!
REALLY?!?
LET'S HAVE A PIC-NIC!
LATER...
SUMMER AND FRIENDS! NOW MY PASTIME IS JUST PERFECT!
AND WE'LL LOVE TO SPEND OUR TIME WITH YOU!

The End

ICE CREAM SMEARS

Manuscript: Tea Orsi; Layout: Emilio Urbano; Cleanup: Nicoletta Baldari; Color: Dario Calabria

The End

SMART PAINTINGS

HMMM... THERE ARE SOME GOOD FRIENDS MISSING FROM OUR ART GALLERY.

I CAN FIX THAT!

ANNA REACHES HER FRIENDS, THE TROLLS, BUT...

OOOPS! I THINK I'LL NEED A MUCH LARGER PARCHMENT...

I THINK I KNOW WHAT TO DO!

LATER...

NOW ALL OF OUR FRIENDS ARE IN THE GALLERY!

Manuscript: Tea Orsi; Layout: Emilio Urbano; Cleanup: Rosa La Barbera; Color: Dario Calabria

The End

KRISTOFF'S SPEECH

anuscript: Alessandro Ferrari; Layout: Alberto Zanon; Cleanup: Veronica Di Lorenzo; Color: Dario Calabria

THREE THRUMMING THIRSTY THIEVES THRUSTING THREE THRONES THROUGH A THRIVING OF THORNS!

I FORBEAR, BUT I CAN'T BEAR TO HEAR WITH A BEAR IN MY EAR THIS YEAR!

I HOPE I CAN. I MEAN, I KNOW I CAN. THANK YOU, ANNA.

REMEMBER... EVERY WORD COUNTS! AND DON'T FORGET TO BREATHE!

HONORED GUESTS...

... WELCOME TO ARENDELLE!

YEAH!

GOOD JOB KRISTOFF!

YOU'RE THE BEST!

WAIT, THAT WAS YOUR SPEECH... THREE WORDS?

I KNOW, BUT EVERY WORD COUNTS.

The End

184

SEA RESCUE

Part 1

ELSA, ANNA, AND FRIENDS ARE SAILING BACK TO ARENDELLE AFTER A TRIP, WHEN...

LOOKS LIKE A STORM IS COMING!

WHOOOOSH

SPLOOOSH

I HOPE WE REACH THE HARBOR SOON!

LOOK! OVER THERE!

Manuscript: Tea Orsi; Layout: Gianluca Barone; Clean: Benedetta Barone and MichelAngela World; Color: MichelAngela World

YOU'RE RIGHT, OLAF. IT'S NEAR THE CLIFFS!

LET ME SEE...

"OH NO! I THINK IT'S A DOLPHIN... IN TROUBLE!"

SWOOOSH

SPLASH

"IT LOOKS LIKE HE'S TANGLED IN A FISHING NET, AND THE NET IS CAUGHT ON THE ROCKS..."

THE DOLPHIN IS TRAPPED!

WE HAVE TO DO SOMETHING!

HOW CAN WE HELP HIM?

FIRST OF ALL, WE NEED TO REACH HIM!

CAPTAIN, CAN WE SAIL CLOSER TO THOSE CLIFFS?

IT'S TOO RISKY, YOUR MAJESTY! WE HAVE TO GET BACK TO THE HARBOR BEFORE THE STORM BREAKS...

OH NO! WE CAN'T LEAVE HIM THERE!

HE'LL BE LONELY!

NHOOOOSH

MAYBE I CAN KEEP HIM COMPANY!

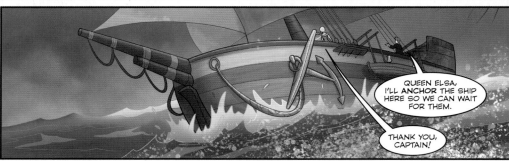

WILL ANNA AND KRISTOFF FREE THE DOLPHIN? YOU'LL FIND OUT IN THE SECOND PART OF THIS EXCITING ADVENTURE!

End Of Part 1

Sea Rescue

ANNA AND KRISTOFF VENTURED INTO THE STORMY SEA TO RESCUE A DOLPHIN IN TROUBLE, AND NOW...

WE'RE ALMOST THERE!

BUT THE CURRENT IS SO STRONG IT'S PUSHING US TOWARDS THE CLIFFS!

WHOOOSH

THEY ARE SO BRAVE!

YES THEY ARE OLAF; THE CURRENT IS REALLY POWERFUL!

THEN...

I'LL TRY TO REACH THE NET FROM THE CLIFF!

GOOD PLAN! I'LL TAKE CARE OF THE BOAT!

GASP!

WHOOOSH

anuscript: Tea Orsi; Layout: Gianluca Barone; Clean: Benedetta Barone and MichelAngela World; Color: MichelAngela World

OUCH! THE WAVES ARE TOO STRONG!

YIKES!

THEN, KRISTOFF TRIES AGAIN...

LET'S SEE IF I CAN UNTANGLE THE NET...

SPLOOSH

BUT...

KRISTOFF, WATCH OUT! THERE'S ANOTHER WAVE COMING!

SWOOOSH

GASP!

SPLOOSH

WHOOOSH

KRISTOFF! I'M COMING!

190

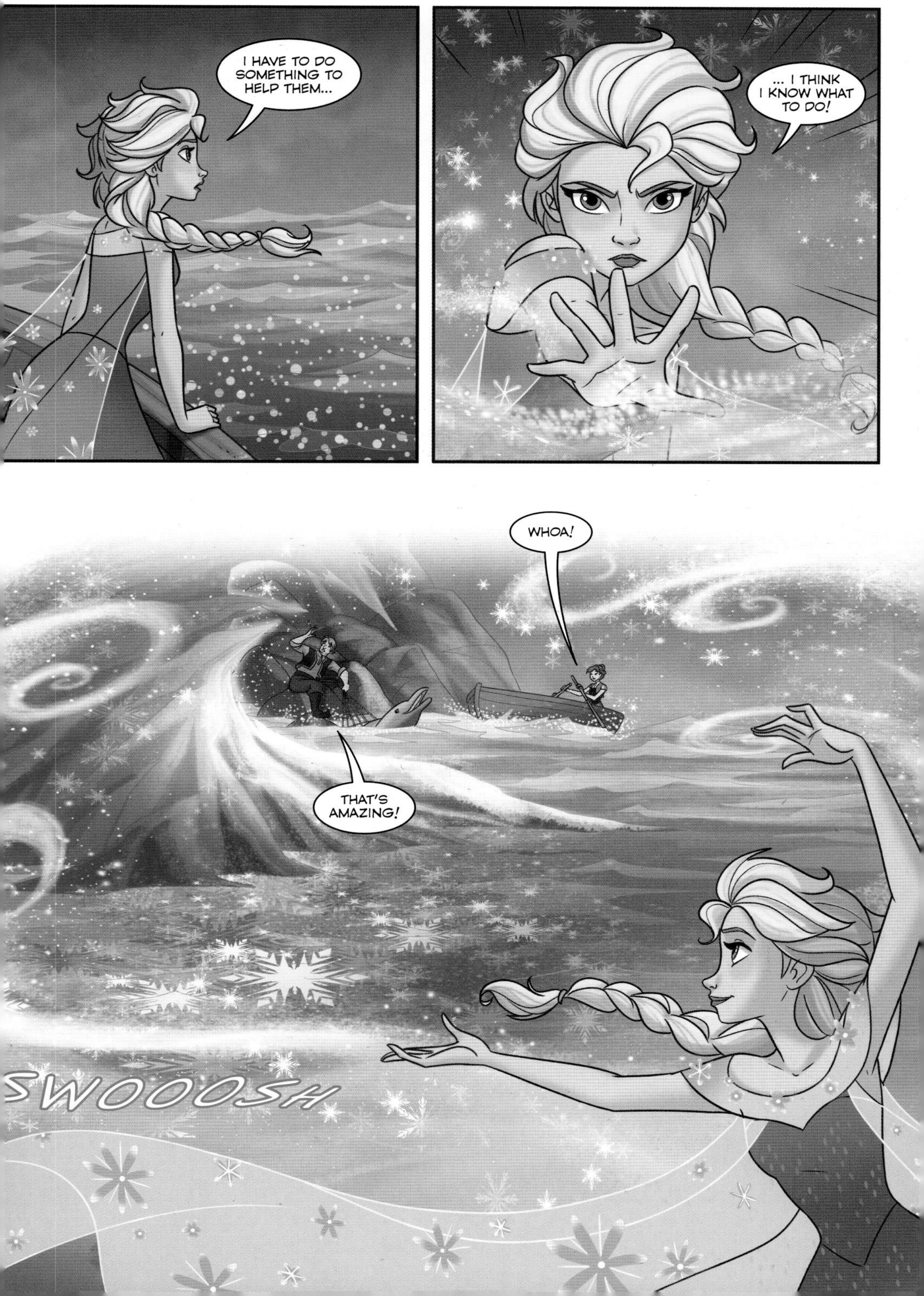
I HAVE TO DO SOMETHING TO HELP THEM...
... I THINK I KNOW WHAT TO DO!
WHOA!
THAT'S AMAZING!
SWOOOSH

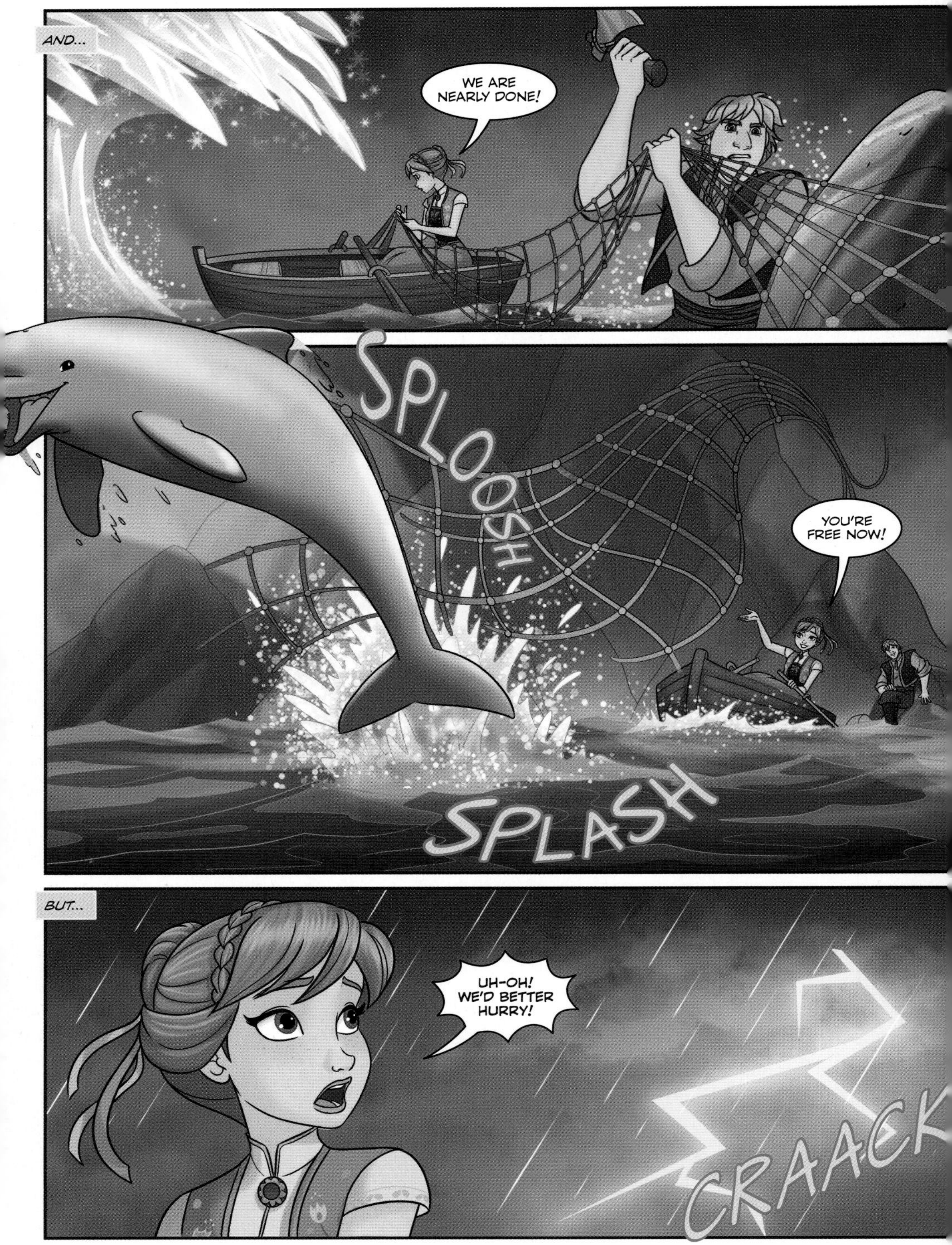
AND...
WE ARE NEARLY DONE!
SPLOOOSH
YOU'RE FREE NOW!
SPLASH
BUT...
UH-OH! WE'D BETTER HURRY!
CRAACK

ANNA AND KRISTOFF SAIL BACK TO THE SHIP AND GET ON BOARD...

THE DOLPHIN WAS HAPPY TO BE FREE!

ALL THANKS TO ELSA'S HELP!

LOOK! I THINK OUR FRIEND IS GUIDING US BACK TO SHORE!

MAYBE HE WANTS TO THANK US FOR FREEING HIM!

CAN WE FOLLOW HIM, CAPTAIN?

SURE! I'VE NEVER HAD SUCH AN EXPERIENCED GUIDE!

AND...

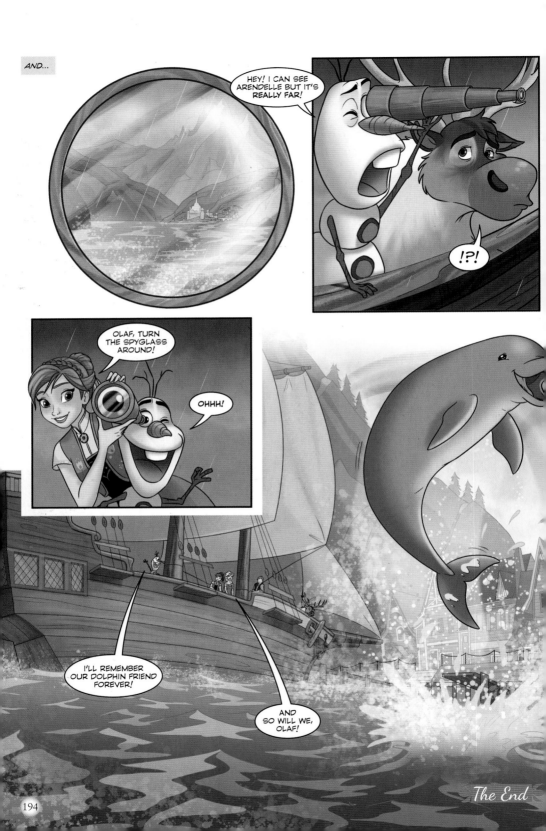

HEY! I CAN SEE ARENDELLE BUT IT'S REALLY FAR!

!?!

OLAF, TURN THE SPYGLASS AROUND!

OHHH!

I'LL REMEMBER OUR DOLPHIN FRIEND FOREVER!

AND SO WILL WE, OLAF!

The End

WARM HUGS FOR EVERYONE

anuscript: Tea Orsi; Layout: Emilio Urbano; Cleanup: Rosa La Barbera; Color: Dario Calabria

The End

THE TALKING HIDING PLACE

OLAF IS PLAYING HIDE-'N-SEEK WITH HIS TROLL FRIENDS...

ONE, TWO, THREE...

I HAVE TO BE QUICK!

NO ONE WILL SEE ME HERE!

HI, OLAF!

HUH?!? HELLO!

HOW ARE YOU DOIN'?

OLAAAF! I FOUND YOU!

!?!

NEXT TIME YOU MIGHT WANT TO HIDE IN THE TREES!

Manuscript: Tea Orsi; Layout: Emilio Urbano; Cleanup: Letizia Algeri; Color: Dario Calabria

The End

THE STRANGEST SHEEP!

cript: Tea Orsi; Layout: Emilio Urbano; Cleanup: Benedetta Barone; Color: Dario Calabria

MARSHMALLOOOOW, LITTLE BROOOTHERS!

THAT'S NOT A SHEEP! IT IS...

OOOOOOH!

POING POING POING POING POING POING POING

HAHA! IT WAS JUST THE SNOWGIES GIVING MARSHMALLOW A BIG HUG!

AND NOW IT'S OLAF'S TURN!

The End

ICE LESSON

ONE DAY, IN ARENDELLE...

GOOD MORNING, CHILDREN!

GOOD MORNING, QUEEN ELSA!

GOOD MORNING, PRINCESS ANNA!

AS YOU ALL KNOW, TODAY KRISTOFF WILL TALK ABOUT HIS JOB AS AN ICE HARVESTER...

GOOD MORNING, EVERYONE! ARE YOU READY FOR SOME ICE LEARNING?

anuscript: Tea Orsi; Layout: Alberto Zanon; Cleanup: Letizia Algeri; Color: MichelAngela World

TOUGH CROWD, HUH?

DON'T WORRY, THEY JUST NEED TO WARM UP. THEY'RE GONNA LOVE YOU!

LET'S START WITH THE BASICS, OKAY?

ICE HARVESTING IS A SCIENCE THAT REQUIRES SKILL AND A DEEP KNOWLEDGE OF...

YES?

EXCUSE ME, SIR!

HAVE YOU EVER CUT AN ICE BLOCK THIS BIG?

WHAT ABOUT ONE AS BIG AS A REINDEER?

HOW ABOUT AS BIG AS A SAUNA?

AND AS BIG AS A CASTLE?

WAIT, WAIT! ICE HARVESTING IS HARD WORK... I'M GOING TO TELL YOU HOW IT'S DONE AND...

CAN WE SEE THE BIG ICE BLOCKS INSTEAD?

DID YOU BRING THEM?

HOW BIG IS YOUR SLEIGH?

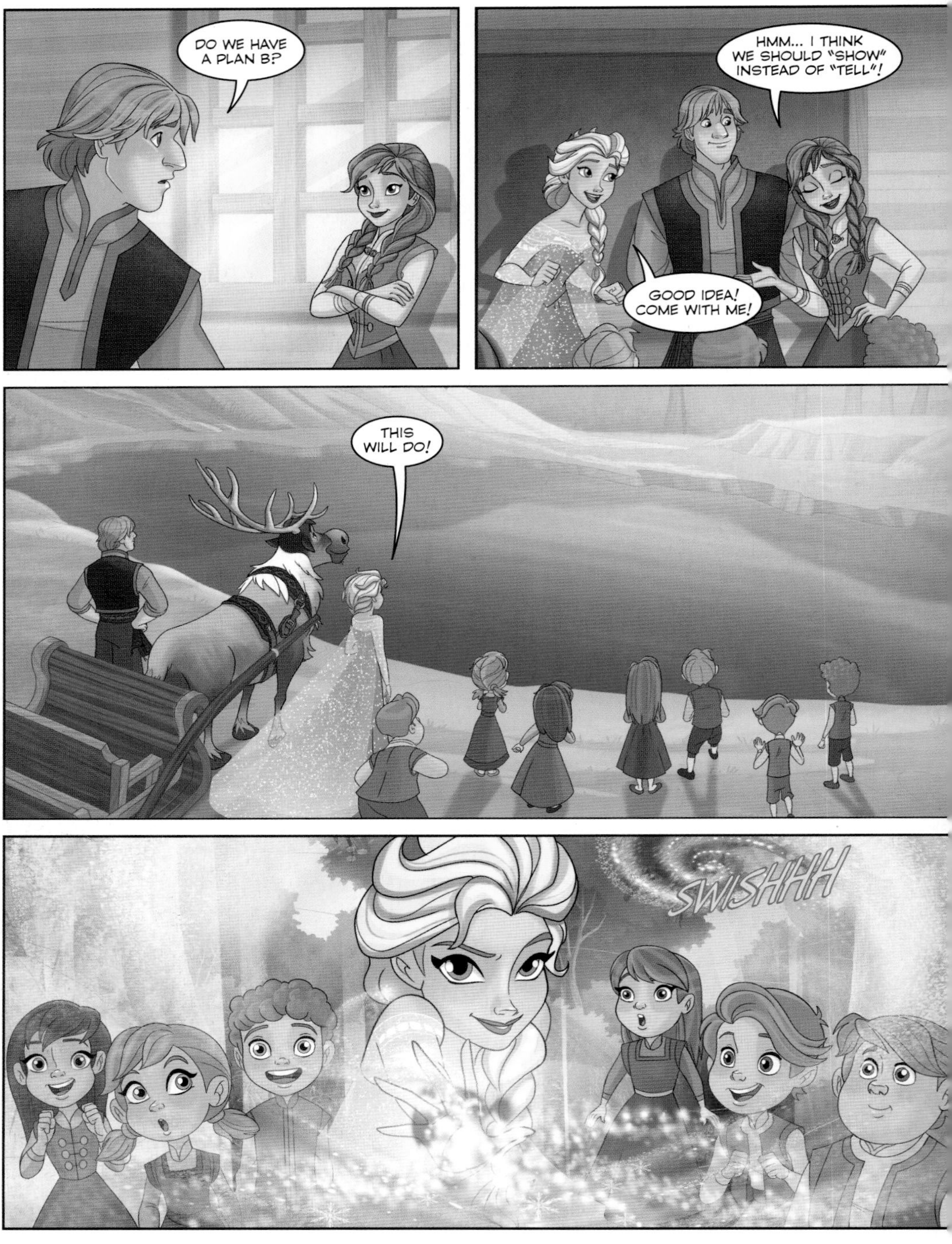

DO WE HAVE A PLAN B?
HMM... I THINK WE SHOULD "SHOW" INSTEAD OF "TELL"!
GOOD IDEA! COME WITH ME!
THIS WILL DO!
SWISHHH

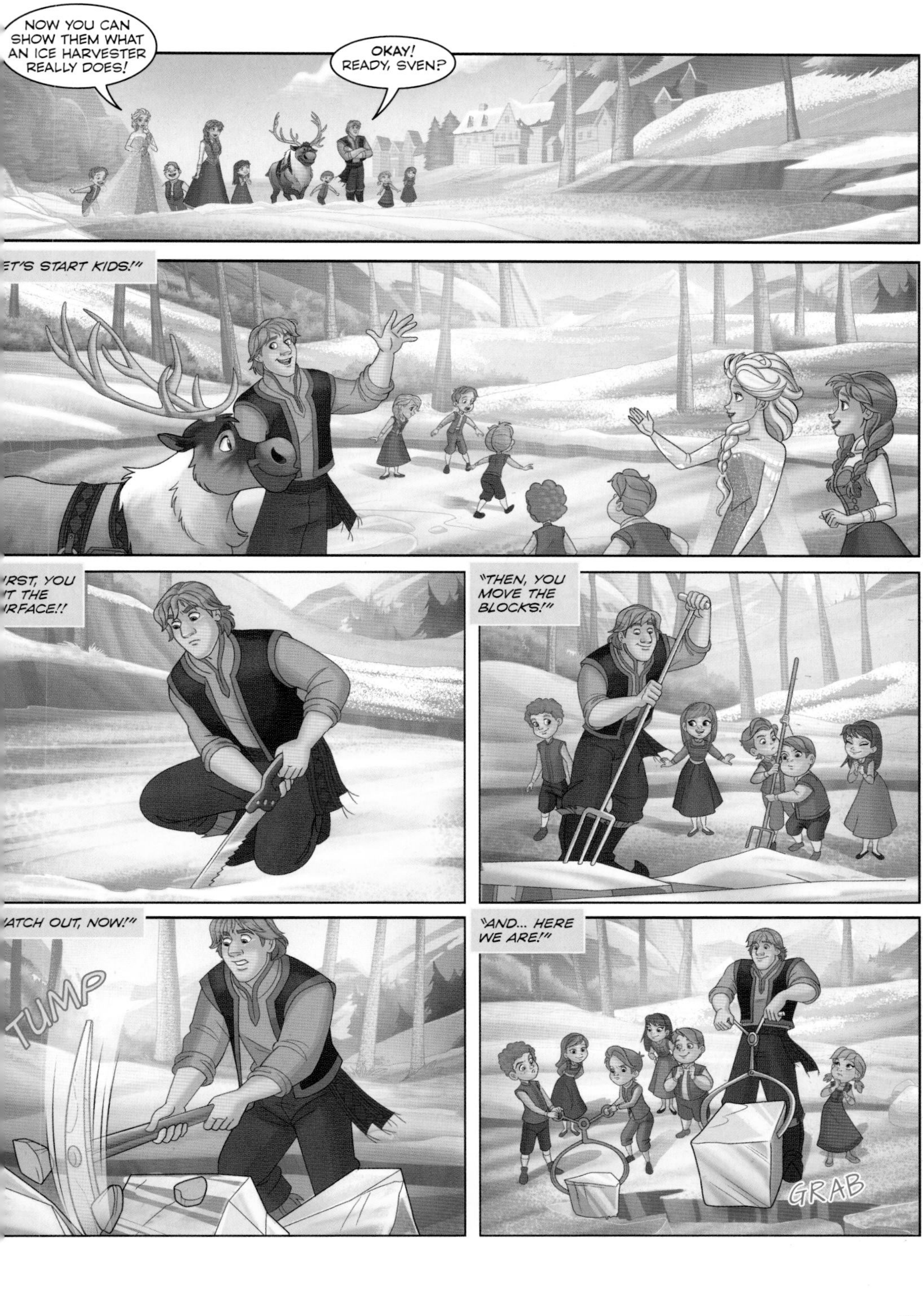
NOW YOU CAN SHOW THEM WHAT AN ICE HARVESTER REALLY DOES!
OKAY! READY, SVEN?
ET'S START KIDS!"
IRST, YOU T THE IRFACE!!
"THEN, YOU MOVE THE BLOCKS!"
ATCH OUT, NOW!"
TUMP
"AND... HERE WE ARE!"
GRAB

AFTER SOME TIME...

WE DID A GREAT JOB!

THIS IS...

... THE MOST INCREDIBLE AMAZING THING EVER!

I WANT TO BECOME LIKE YOU WHEN I GROW UP!

TELL US EVERYTHING ABOUT ICE!

WELL, KRISTOFF... YOU MELTED THE AUDIENCE AFTER ALL!

The End

POINTS OF VIEW

IT'S A PERFECT DAY TO HIKE IN THE MOUNTAINS!

LOOK! THERE'S SOMETHING OVER THERE!

WE COULD SEE IT IF WE HAD A SPYGLASS.

IT'S SO TEENY-TINY!

HERE YOU ARE! THIS MIGHT DO THE TRICK!

OH, THANK YOU, ELSA! I CAN ALMOST SEE IT NOW!

NOW IT'S A LITTLE BIGGER THAN TEENY-TINY!

HOW'S IT NOW?

HUM... ALMOST THERE! IF I COULD JUST ZOOM IN A LITTLE BIT MORE...

YES! NOW IT'S PERFECT!

?

HELLO, LITTLE FRIEND!

YOU MAY NEED A MEGAPHONE FOR THIS!

I'M NOT SURE IT CAN HEAR YOU, OLAF!

!

Manuscript: Valentina Cambi; Layout: Alberto Zanon; Cleanup: Michela Frare and Letizia Algeri; Ink: Michela Frare; Color: MichelAngela World

The End

SPRING TROLLS

TONIGHT ANNA AND ELSA ARE VISITING THE TROLLS...

HERE'S A SMALL SPRING GIFT FOR YOU!

YOU CAN WEAR IT ON YOUR HEAD!

THIS IS BEAUTIFUL!

YEAH, I LOVE IT!

I CAN'T WAIT TO SHOW THIS TO KRISTOFF AND SVEN!

WELL, I THINK THEY HAVE SOMETHING TO SHOW YOU AS WELL!

OH YEAH! WE JUST GOT OUR SMALL SPRING PRESENTS TOO!

WHOA!

SPRING HAS DEFINITELY **SPRUN** THANKS, BULDA

Manuscript: Tea Orsi; Layout: Emilio Urbano; Cleanup: Chatal Christine; Color: Stefania Santi

The End

A Mysterious Invitation

ANNA IS READY TO TAKE A WALK, WHEN...

HUH?! WHAT'S A BASKET DOING THERE?

A MESSAGE?

In the woods...

IN THE WOODS?!

ANNA! LOOK! I'VE FOUND SOMETHING NEAR THE WINDOW!

HEY! YOU'VE GOT ONE TOO!

In the woods...

THERE WAS PART OF A MESSAGE INSIDE IT!

...You'll find...

anuscript: Tea Orsi; Layout: Nicoletta Baldari; Cleanup: Veronica Di lorenzo; Color: Patrizia Zangrilli and Antonia Angrisani

IT LOOKS LIKE THEY GO TOGETHER...

WHO WROTE THEM?

In the woods...

...You'll find...

LOOK WHAT I FOUND! WHAT DOES IT SAY?

IT WAS SURELY THE SAME PERSON, BUT...HUH?!?

IT WAS NEAR THE FLOWERS! I ALWAYS SAY HI TO THEM IN THE MORNING.

I CAN'T BELIEVE IT! YOU FOUND ONE TOO!

AW, I CAN'T READ IT EITHER!

MAYBE IT'S WRITTEN IN CODE...

ALMOST... THIS MESSAGE IS STAINED!

...The

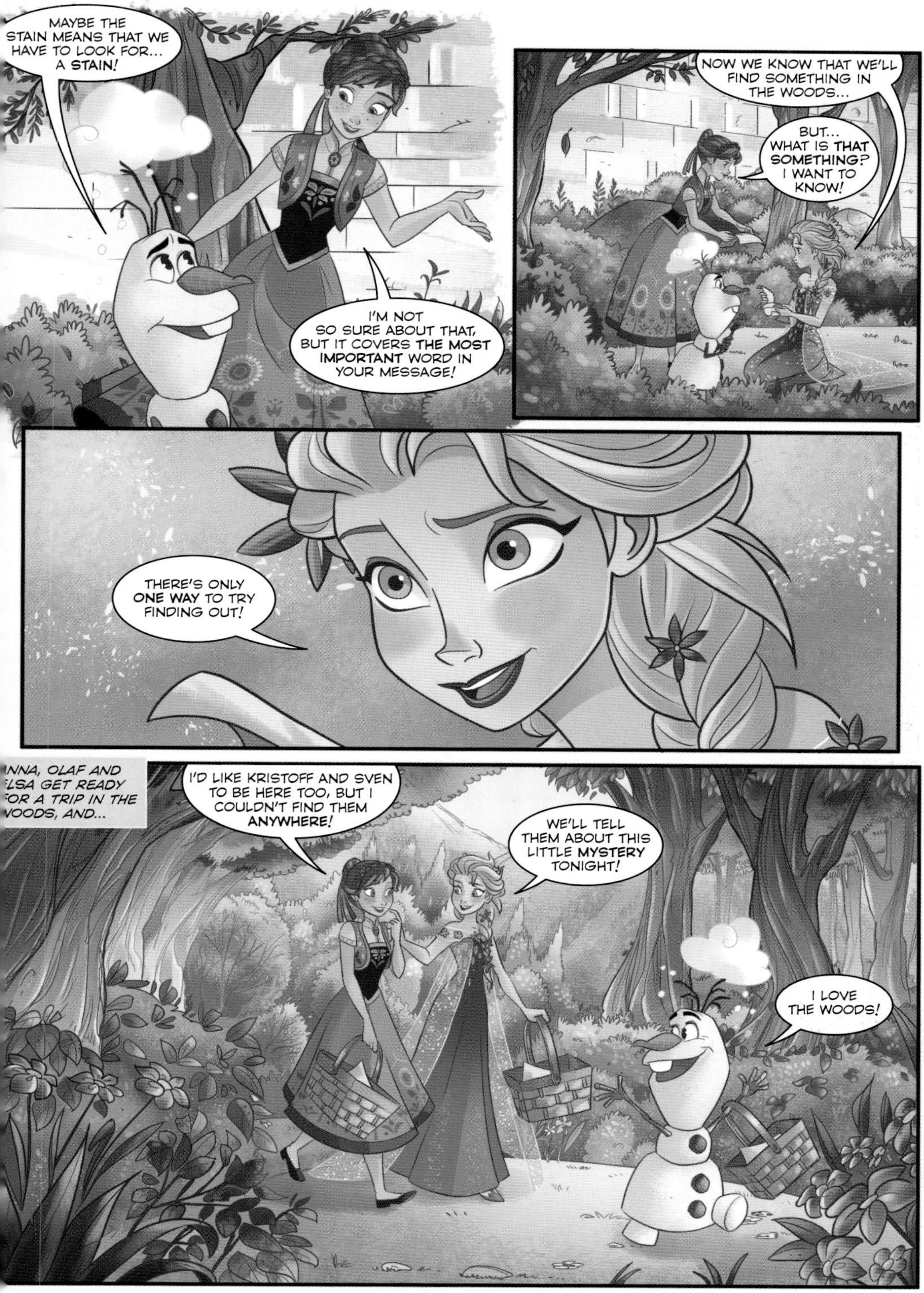
MAYBE THE STAIN MEANS THAT WE HAVE TO LOOK FOR... A STAIN!
I'M NOT SO SURE ABOUT THAT, BUT IT COVERS THE MOST IMPORTANT WORD IN YOUR MESSAGE!
NOW WE KNOW THAT WE'LL FIND SOMETHING IN THE WOODS...
BUT... WHAT IS THAT SOMETHING? I WANT TO KNOW!
THERE'S ONLY ONE WAY TO TRY FINDING OUT!
NNA, OLAF AND LSA GET READY OR A TRIP IN THE OODS, AND...
I'D LIKE KRISTOFF AND SVEN TO BE HERE TOO, BUT I COULDN'T FIND THEM ANYWHERE!
WE'LL TELL THEM ABOUT THIS LITTLE MYSTERY TONIGHT!
I LOVE THE WOODS!

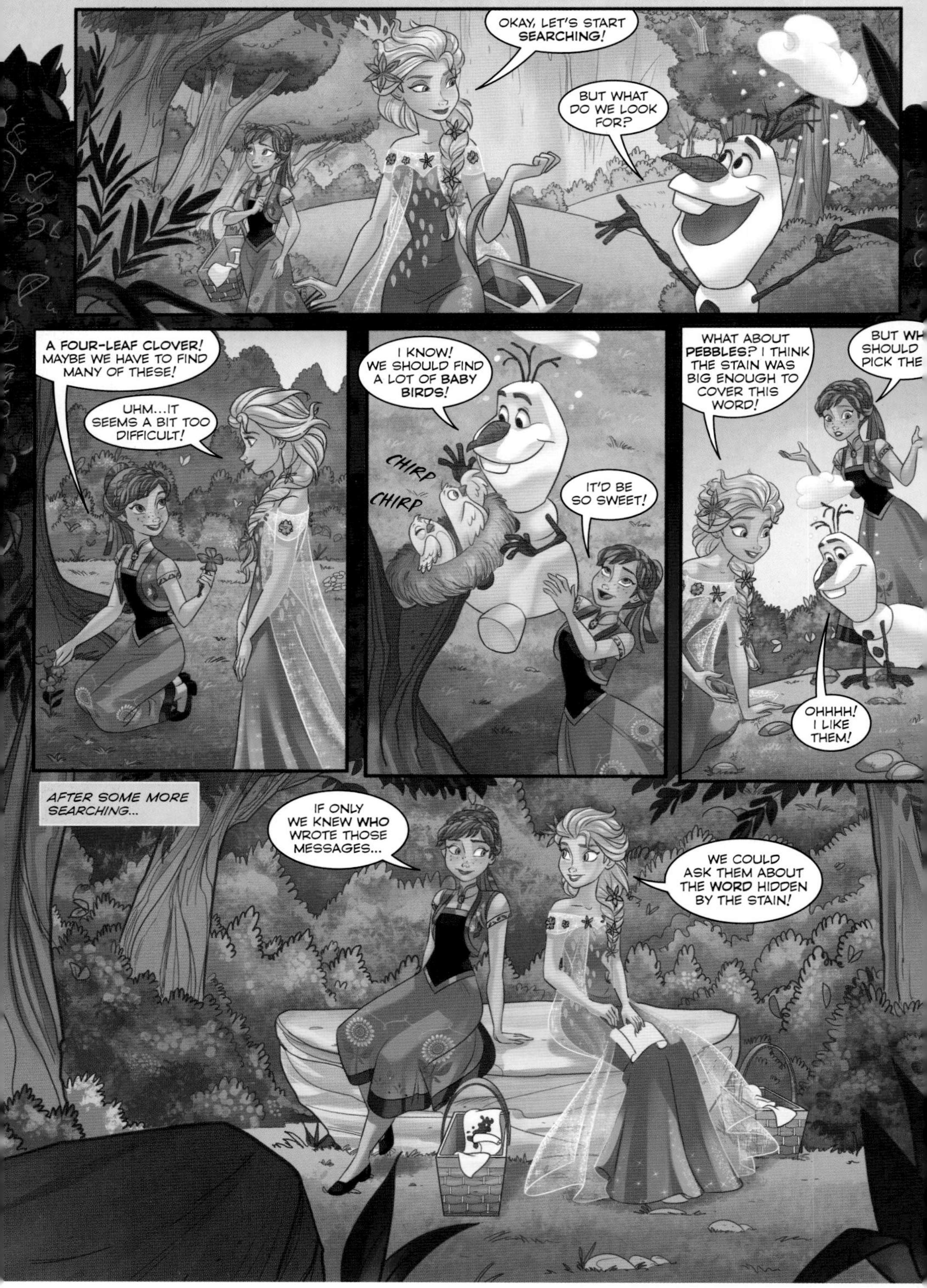

OKAY, LET'S START SEARCHING!
BUT WHAT DO WE LOOK FOR?
A FOUR-LEAF CLOVER! MAYBE WE HAVE TO FIND MANY OF THESE!
UHM...IT SEEMS A BIT TOO DIFFICULT!
I KNOW! WE SHOULD FIND A LOT OF BABY BIRDS!
CHIRP
CHIRP
IT'D BE SO SWEET!
WHAT ABOUT PEBBLES? I THINK THE STAIN WAS BIG ENOUGH TO COVER THIS WORD!
OHHHH! I LIKE THEM!
AFTER SOME MORE SEARCHING...
IF ONLY WE KNEW WHO WROTE THOSE MESSAGES...
WE COULD ASK THEM ABOUT THE WORD HIDDEN BY THE STAIN!

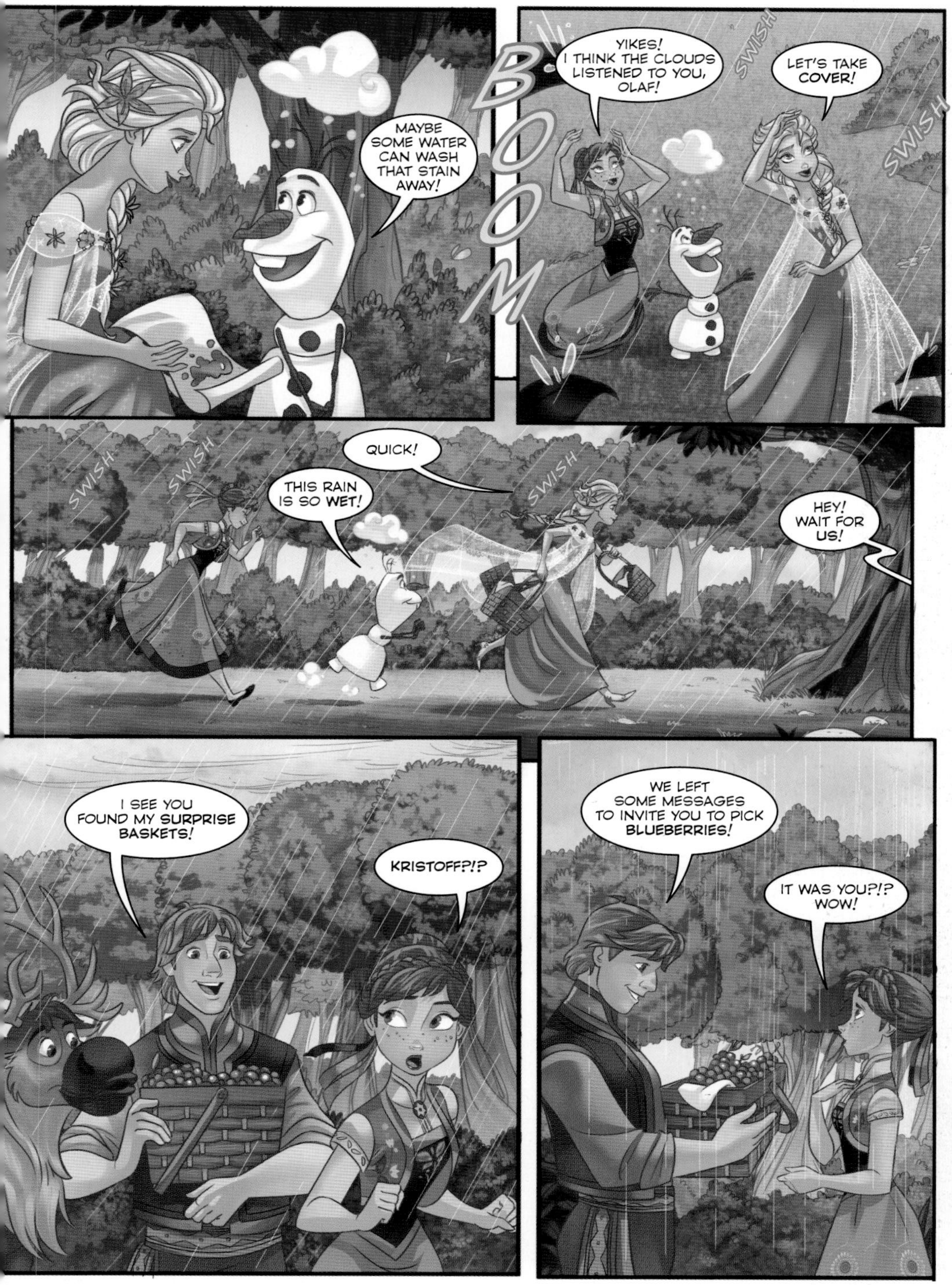

MAYBE SOME WATER CAN WASH THAT STAIN AWAY!
BOOOM
YIKES! I THINK THE CLOUDS LISTENED TO YOU, OLAF!
SWISH
LET'S TAKE COVER!
SWISH
SWISH
SWISH
SWISH
QUICK!
THIS RAIN IS SO WET!
SWISH
HEY! WAIT FOR US!
I SEE YOU FOUND MY SURPRISE BASKETS!
KRISTOFF?!?
WE LEFT SOME MESSAGES TO INVITE YOU TO PICK BLUEBERRIES!
IT WAS YOU?!? WOW!

THE GROUP TAKES SHELTER, AND...

SO THE PURPLE STAIN WAS JUST BLUEBERRY JUICE!

WHICH STAIN?

THIS ONE! DID YOU WANT US TO GUESS THE WORD BLUEBERRIES?

NO, BUT NOW I REMEMBER SOMETHING...

!

...The

"BEFORE SVEN AND I PLACED THE BASKETS IN THE DIFFERENT SPOTS, HE TASTED SOME BLUEBERRIES..."

MUNCH MUNCH

"I'M SURE IT WAS AN ACCIDENT, BUT I DIDN'T NOTICE ANYTHING!"

WELL... NEXT TIME I'LL GO FOR A TRADITIONAL INVITATION. OKAY, BUDDY?

NO WAY! WE HAD SO MUCH FUN!

AND NOW THAT THE SUN IS BACK, WE CAN FINALLY FILL OUR BASKETS!

The End

212

ICE PALACE SOUND

ELSA INVITED HER FRIENDS TO THE ICE PALACE FOR A SPECIAL HOLIDAY CELEBRATION...

I CAN'T WAIT TO FIND OUT MORE ABOUT ELSA'S SURPRISE!

ME TOO!

SURPRISES ARE ALWAYS SO SURPRISING!

LET'S GO IN NOW! YOU ARE MAKING ME EVEN MORE CURIOUS!

WELCOME, EVERYONE! LET ME INTRODUCE YOU TO THE MOST FESTIVE CHOIR EVER...

MARSHMALLOW AND THE SNOWGIES!

Manuscript: Tea Orsi; Layout: Alberto Zanon; Cleanup: Nicoletta Baldari; Color: Manuela Nerolini

The End

A Carrot Surprise

Manuscript: Tea Orsi; Layout and cleanup: Nicoletta Baldari; Color: Dario Calabri

The End

How to Scare a Troll

VALLEY OF THE TROLLS, KRISTOFF HAS JUST FOUND HIS OLD FRIENDS...

KRISTOFF! YOU'RE BACK!

LET'S PLAY A SCARY GAME WITH KRISTOFF!

YOU CAN'T, HE'S TOO BUSY NOW!

PLEASE! KRISTOFF'S SCARY GAMES ARE AMAZING!

WE LOVE THEM!

I KNOW, KIDS. BUT YOU'VE GOT TO BE PATIENT...

I CAN PLAY WITH YOU!

?

I KNOW A LOT OF SCARY GAMES!

REALLY?

Writer: Alessandro Ferrari; Artist: Iboix Estudi; Colorist: Charles Pickens; Letterer: Patrick Brosseau

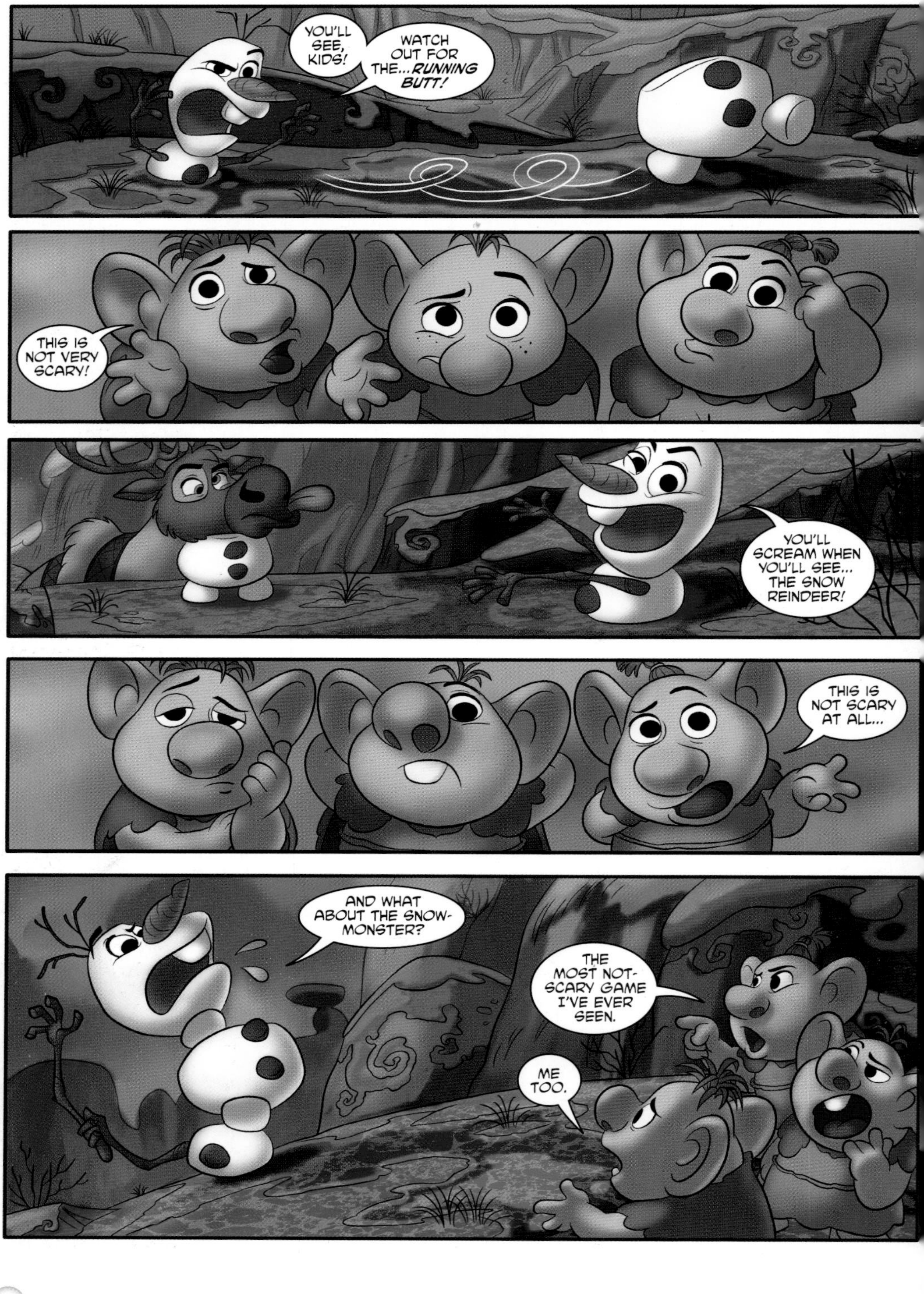
YOU'LL SEE, KIDS!
WATCH OUT FOR THE...RUNNING BUTT!
THIS IS NOT VERY SCARY!
YOU'LL SCREAM WHEN YOU'LL SEE... THE SNOW REINDEER!
THIS IS NOT SCARY AT ALL...
AND WHAT ABOUT THE SNOW-MONSTER?
THE MOST NOT-SCARY GAME I'VE EVER SEEN.
ME TOO.

LET'S GO, SVEN. I'M NOT SCARY ENOUGH FOR THEM...

HUH? WHY AM I STILL HERE?

WOW! THIS GREY SNOW IS NOT LEAVING ME!

I THINK... YOU MUST PULL... HARDER, SVEN!

SPLASH

DEFINITELY HARDER...

YES! WE'RE... ALMOST...

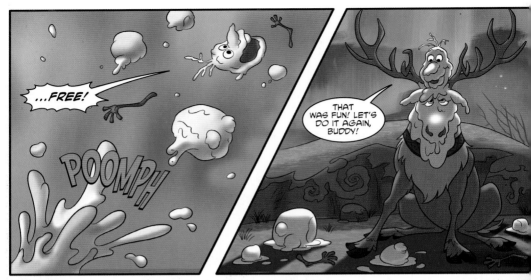

...FREE!

POOMPH

THAT WAS FUN! LET'S DO IT AGAIN, BUDDY!

?

AHHHHH!

SCARY MONSTER! SCARY MONSTER!

THE MOST SCARY MONSTER EVER!

WELL...IT WASN'T THAT HARD, WAS IT?

The End

THE CARROT GUARD

ELSA HAS JUST GONE OUT, WHEN...

HEY, SVEN!

LATER, ANNA GOES OUT TOO AND...

HUH?!?

AT SUNSET, WHEN THEY COME BACK TOGETHER...

I CAN'T BELIEVE SVEN IS STILL THERE!

YEAH, I WAS ABOUT TO SAY THE SAME THING!

HE'S BEEN STANDING THERE FOR HOURS!

anuscript: Tea Orsi; Layout: Emilio Urbano;
eanup: Veronica Di Lorenzo; Color: Dario Calabria

219

THE TWO SISTERS GO INSIDE AND ASK KRISTOFF...

WHAT IS SVEN DOING NEAR THAT PATCH OF DIRT?

HE SEEMS SO FOCUSED!

WELL... WE PLANTED SOME CARROT SEEDS THIS MORNING...

I TOLD HIM THAT IT WILL TAKE TIME FOR THE CARROTS TO GROW, BUT...

"...HE JUST CAN'T WAIT!"

The End

A WARM SIGHT

IT'S THE PERFECT DAY FOR SITTING BY A FIRE, BUT...

AHHH! I'D GIVE YOU A BIG HUG IF I COULD!

ERM... OLAF...

BUT IT'S SO **WARM** AND NICE!

GASP! I'D BETTER CALL ELSA!

ANNA FINDS ELSA IN HER ROOM, AND...

OLAF WANTS TO SIT BY THE FIRE, BUT IT'S TOO HOT!

DON'T WORRY, I KNOW WHAT TO DO!

ELSA DOES HER MAGIC...

SWOOSH

AND SOON...

AH! I LOVE THIS FREEZING WARM FEELING!

YOU REALLY MADE HIM HAPPY, ELSA!

The End

nuscript: Tea Orsi; Layout: Emilio Urbano; anup: Nicoletta Baldari; Color: Dario Calabria

EVERYTHING YOU NEED

THE SUMMER STOCK-UP SALE IS IN THE MAIN SQUARE!

OOOOOOH... WHAT IS A STOCK-UP SALE?

IT'S A SALE WHERE YOU GET EVERYTHING YOU NEED FOR THE WINTER, ALL AT ONCE!

YOU CAN STOCK UP ON CLOTHES, ON FOOD, ON... ERM... CARROTS FOR SVEN...

OH, LOOK! THERE'S OAKEN!

HI OAKEN, SO YOU'RE THE ONLY MERCHANT HAVING A STOCK-UP SALE??

YOU CAN STOCK UP ON EVERYTHING RIGHT HERE!

YEP, JUST OAKEN'S!

Manuscript: Tea Orsi; Layout: Alberto Zanon; Cleanup: Michela Frare and Sara Storino; Ink and Color: MichelAngela World

The End

A SONG FOR SVEN

ANNA HAS A BIG SURPRISE FOR THE VILLAGERS: SHE CREATED A SPECIAL PLACE TO HELP THEM REST AFTER ALL THEIR HARD WORK...

WELCOME TO ARENDELLE'S ONE AND ONLY OASIS OF RELAXATION!

I'D LIKE TO PLAY SOME RELAXING MUSIC FOR YOU ALL.

I WILL SING ONE OF SVEN'S FAVORITE LULLABIES!

Original Story: Erica David; Adaptation: Chantal Pericoli; Layout: Marino Gentile; Clean: Federica Salfo and Sara Storino; Ink: MichelAngela World; Color: Silvano Scolari

There's no deer like a reindeer,
'cause reindeer are the best.
They're loyal friends,
until the end,
who work without much rest...

So if you love your reindeer,
you'll give him lots of care
with carrots, hay
and time for play,
'cause even reindeer
need a day
to just kick up their hooves
and say:
reindeer are the best.

CLAP CLAP

CLAP CLAP

GREAT JOB, KRISTOFF! VERY SOOTHING, ESPECIALLY FOR THE REINDEER!

THAT'S MY GOAL, TO SOOTHE REINDEER AND PEOPLE ALIKE!

ZZZZ

ZZZZZ

ZZZZZZ

ZZZZ

SNORE SNORE

ZZZZ

ZZZZ

YOU MIGHT HAVE DONE TOO GOOD OF A JOB. HAHAHAH!

The End

A Bright Guide

KRISTOFF, SVEN AND OLAF ARE WALKING BACK TO THE CASTLE AFTER A HIKE, BUT...

GASP! I CAN'T SEE ANYTHING!

IS THIS A NEW GAME?!?

NO, OLAF! IT'S FOG, AND IT'S REALLY THICK!

UH?!? I THINK IT'S KIND OF PRETTY!

BUT...HOW WILL WE KNOW WHERE WE ARE GOING?!?

I HAVE AN IDEA!

?!?

AND...

WELL DONE, KRISTOFF! NOW THE FOG IS EVEN PRETTIER!

YEP, THIS WAS DEFINITELY THE **BRIGHTEST** IDEA I'VE EVER HAD!

anuscript: Tea Orsi; Layout: Emilio Urbano; Cleanup: Marino Gentile; Color: Dario Calabria

The End

HEAVY CLIMBING

AH, WE'LL HAVE A WONDERFUL TIME TOGETHER!

SITTING AMONG THE FLOWERS, PLAYING ON THE GRASS...

OH YES, IT WILL BE GREAT... ONCE WE GET...TO REACH THE TOP!

HUH?!? YOUR BASKETS LOOK SO HEAVY!

ERM... WE THOUGHT... WE WOULD BE REALLY HUNGRY...AFTER THE HIKE!

BUT MAYBE WE OVERDID IT A BIT!

COME ON! THINK HOW EASY IT WILL BE GOING DOWN THE MOUNTAIN ONCE WE EAT ALL THIS FOOD.

THEN I'VE GOT A BETTER IDEA... LET'S EAT EVERYTHING NOW!

JUST KIDDING! TEE HEE!

Manuscript: Tea Orsi; Layout: Marino Gentile; Cleanup: Marino Gentile;
Ink: Cristina Stella; Color: Patrizia Zangrilli

The End

A Beautiful "Oops"

anuscript: Tea Orsi; Layout: Alberto Zanon; Cleanup: Letizia Algeri; Color: MichelAngela word

... YOU ACTUALLY GAVE ME A **WONDERFUL** IDEA!

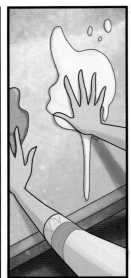

SWOOSH

SWISH

AND...

TA-DAH! WITHOUT YOUR HELP MY PAINTING WOULD HAVE NEVER BEEN THIS AMAZING!

I LOVE IT! BUT... **WHAT** IS IT?

IT COULD BE WHATEVER YOU WANT! JUST LOOK AT IT AND IMAGINE!

IT LOOKS JUST LIKE **SUMMER** TO ME!

LOVELY! AND I THINK I CAN GUESS WHAT SVEN SEES...

The End

A Tough Delivery

OUTSIDE IT'S SNOWING, AND...

I WON AGAIN!

YOU ARE SO GOOD AT THIS GAME, ANNA!

YES, THIS IS DEFINITELY YOUR LUCKY DAY!

KNOCK KNOCK

PLEASE, COME IN!

QUEEN ELSA, THE VILLAGE BAKER NEEDS TO TALK TO YOU!

I'M SORRY TO BOTHER YOU, YOUR MAJESTY, BUT IT'S AN EMERGENCY!

I BAKED SOME BREAD FOR MY COUSINS, WHO LIVE UP ON THE MOUNTAINS...

anuscript: Tea Orsi; Layout: Emilio Urbano; Cleanup: Manuela Razzi; Color: Maria Claudia Di Genova

...BUT THE ROAD IS BLOCKED BY THE REMAINS OF A SMALL **AVALANCHE** AND I CAN'T REACH THEIR HOUSE!

THEY LIVE IN A VERY ISOLATED AREA AND ARE RUNNING OUT OF FOOD SUPPLIES!

THEY'RE GOING TO **STARVE** IF THEY DON'T GET HELP!

THEY HAVE LITTLE **CHILDREN** TOO!

DON'T WORRY, WE'LL SET OFF IMMEDIATELY, AND WE'LL DO OUR BEST TO REACH THEM!

THANK YOU, YOUR MAJESTY! I'LL GO AND GET THE **PROVISIONS** I PACKED FOR THEM!

I WILL HELP YOU!

WE NEED TO GET READY AS **QUICKLY** AS POSSIBLE!

LET'S PREPARE THE SLEIGH!

THANK YOU... AND BE SAFE!

WE WILL!

SEE YOU SOON!

BAKER

FLOWERS

THESE SUPPLIES LOOK **HEAVY**!

THEY **ARE**, OLAF!

BUT THERE ARE ALSO A LOT OF CARROTS FOR OUR GREAT SVEN!

!

DO YOU HAVE A **PLAN** TO GO PAST THE BLOCKED ROAD?

NOT YET, BUT WE'LL FIND A **WAY**. THAT FAMILY NEEDS OUR HELP!

LOOK! THERE'S A NEW **MOUNTAIN** IN THE MIDDLE OF THE PATH!

YEP, A MOUNTAIN OF SNOW CAUSED BY THE AVALANCHE.

HMMM... I DIDN'T EXPECT IT TO BE THAT BIG...

MAYBE WE CAN CLIMB OVER IT!

OH...MAYBE NOT! WE CAN'T CARRY ALL THE STUFF!

I'LL TRY DIGGING A PASSAGE THROUGH IT!

SWOOSH

BUT...

THE SNOW IS TOO HARD!

SDENG

THANK YOU, KRISTOFF! YOU JUST GAVE ME AN IDEA!

WHOOOSH

AND A LITTLE TOUCH OF ICE TO MAKE EVERYTHING MORE SOLID!

YOUR MAGIC IS AMAZING, ELSA!

OF COURSE IT IS!

SO...

WE'LL REACH THE BAKER'S FAMILY SOON!

YOU'RE A GENIUS, ELSA!

SHE ALWAYS KNOWS WHAT TO DO IN TRICKY SITUATIONS!

WHEN IT STARTS
GETTING DARK...

LOOK! **THAT** MUST BE THE HOUSE WE ARE LOOKING FOR!

WE FOUND THEM!

YOUR COUSIN WAS REALLY WORRIED FOR YOU, SO HE SENT YOU SOME SUPPLIES!

THANK YOU! THE KIDS WERE SO HUNGRY. WE DIDN'T KNOW WHAT TO DO...

OOOOOH!

YOU MUST BE TIRED AND IT'S STARTING TO SNOW AGAIN! PLEASE, COME IN!

WITH PLEASURE!

AND...

HOW DID YOU MANAGE TO TRAVEL PAST THE AVALANCHE?!

OH, IT WAS QUITE AN ADVENTURE!

BUT IT MAKES FOR AN EXCELLENT START TO OUR **WINTER** HOLIDAYS!

The End

CREEPY SHADOWS

IT SEEMED LIKE A QUIET EVENING IN TROLL VALLEY, UNTIL...

AHHH!

A MONSTEEEEEEER!

HELLO! THE FIRST SHOW IS ABOUT A SNOW UNICORN...

THE SHOW HASN'T EVEN STARTED! WHERE DID EVERYONE GO?

anuscript: Tea Orsi; Layout: Alberto Zanon; Cleanup: Rosa La Barbera; Color: Antonella Angrisani

The End

A Cold Check

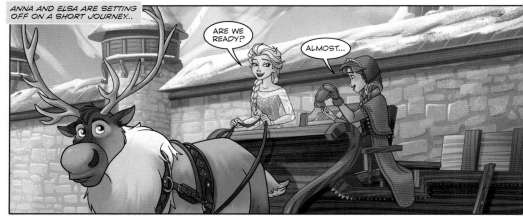

ANNA AND ELSA ARE SETTING OFF ON A SHORT JOURNEY...

ARE WE READY?

ALMOST...

WHAT DOES THAT DO?

I DON'T KNOW.

I SAW KRISTOFF DO IT BEFORE A JOURNEY. IT LOOKED IMPORTANT.

AND... HAVE YOU LEARNED ANYTHING?

YES, NOW I KNOW THAT YOU SHOULDN'T LICK YOUR FINGER AND EXPOSE IT TO THE COLD.

Original Story by Erica David from the book *The Arendelle Cup*; Adaptation by Tea Orsi; Layout: Alberto Zanon; Cleanup: Letizia Algeri; Color: MichelAngela World

The End

ROLE CHANGE

DO YOU REMEMBER WHEN I USED TO **WAKE** YOU UP TO MAKE SNOWMEN?

HOW COULD I FORGET?

OU WERE *ALWAYS* CALLING ME THE MIDDLE OF THE *NIGHT!"*

THE SKY IS AWAKE! YOU SHOULD **WAKE** UP TOO!

ANNA?!?

IT WAS SO MUCH FUN. LET'S DO THAT **AGAIN!**

ERM... I DON'T THINK IT WILL BE **POSSIBLE,** ANNA...

WHY?

WELL...SOME THINGS HAVE CHANGED...

ANNA! IT'S TIME TO WAKE UP! ANNAAAA!

ZZZZZ... I'M COMIN' ....ZZZZ

anuscript: Tea Orsi; Layout: Alberto Zanon; Cleanup: Marino Gentile; Color: MichelAngela World

The End